"And Those Special Memories Are In Sophie's Attic, Tucked Deep In Your Heart?"

Tyson asked quietly.

"Yes," Sophie replied. "That's exactly where they are." She hesitated a moment. "And you? Do you have a Tyson's attic?"

"No."

"It's never too late to discover it's there."

"I just... I just wouldn't have anything to put in it, Sophie."

"Yes, you would," she said softly. "You simply don't realize that you already do."

"Maybe."

They continued to look directly into each other's eyes, a half a room apart. Yet the distance between them seemed somehow to disappear, even though neither moved. Sensuality was heightened, becoming a nearly palpable entity. Hearts began to race, heat began to churn within them, desire began to consume them..

Dear Reader:

Welcome to Silhouette Desire – provocative, compelling, contemporary love stories written by and for today's woman. These are stories to treasure.

Each and every Silhouette Desire is a wonderful romance in which the emotional and the sensual go hand in hand. When you open a Desire, you enter a whole new world – a world that has, naturally, a perfect hero just waiting to whisk you away! A Silhouette Desire can be light-hearted or serious, but it will always be satisfying.

We hope you enjoy this Silhouette today – and will go on to enjoy many more.

Please write to us:

Jane Nicholls
Silhouette Books
PO Box 236
Thornton Road
Croydon
Surrey
CR9 3RU

ROBIN ELLIOTT
SOPHIE'S ATTIC

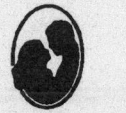

Silhouette Desire

Originally Published by Silhouette Books
a division of
Harlequin Enterprises Ltd.

First published in Great Britain in 1992
by Silhouette Books, Eton House, 18-24 Paradise Road,
Richmond, Surrey TW9 1SR

© Joan Elliott Pickart 1992

Silhouette, Silhouette Desire and Colophon are
Trade Marks of Harlequin Enterprises B.V.

ISBN 0 373 58692 2

22-9212

Made and printed in Great Britain

ROBIN ELLIOTT

lives in a small, charming town in the high pine country of Arizona. She enjoys watching football, attending craft shows on the town square and gardening. Robin also writes under her own name, Joan Elliott Pickart.

Other Silhouette Books by Robin Elliott

Silhouette Desire

Call It Love
To Have It All
Picture of Love
Pennies in the Fountain
Dawn's Gift
Brooke's Chance
Betting Man
Silver Sands
Lost and Found
Out of the Cold

For Tara Hughes Gavin,
with thanks for
keeping the candle
burning in the window

Prologue

Tyson MacDonald strode down the long corridor of the hospital, his numbing fatigue forgotten as he approached the room he sought.

He inwardly groaned as a man in his fifties, wearing a suit and tie, stepped out of the room to block Tyson's way before he could enter. Tyson stopped, his impatience with the delay easily read in his expression.

"MacDonald," the man said, nodding slightly. "They called from downstairs and said you were on your way up. You look like hell. When was the last time you had some decent sleep?"

Tyson shrugged. "I don't know. I just flew through three time zones. I'm not even sure what day this is. I'm in no mood for chitchat, Wilson. I surfaced after a deep-cover assignment to find out that Hank has been in a coma for a month. I want to see him. *Now.*"

"You can see him *after* we talk." Ben Wilson jerked his head toward the door across the hall. "Over there. Come on."

"Damn it, Ben, I want..."

"Now, Tyson."

Muttering an earthy expletive, Tyson entered the indicated room behind Ben. When Ben nodded toward a chair, Tyson shook his head. "I'm so beat that if I sit down I probably won't be able to get up. How's Hank?"

"Nothing has changed. He's in a deep coma. The doctors say we'll have to wait and see. Hank will either come out of it, or stay as he is with machines doing the work his body can't, or he'll die."

"Hell," Tyson said, running one hand over the back of his neck. "I was told that his cover was blown, the assignment was a disaster."

"Yes, thanks to Hank's old nemesis, Jasco."

"Jasco surfaced again?"

"Yep, with knife in hand, per usual, and still looking like the devil himself with that old knife scar down his face, compliments of Hank Clarkson."

"Fill me in."

"It was set, worked out to the last detail. Hank was to meet his contact in that alley and hand over the fountain pen that had the microdot concealed in a carefully constructed cap on the pen. It had taken months of negotiations to get things to come together."

"And?"

"Jasco, and whoever he'd hired on with at the moment, were one step ahead of us. The contact was killed. Jasco and another man were waiting for Hank. The other guy was a shooter. Hank must have resisted—the guy pumped three slugs into him, one of which was a head wound that's causing the coma."

"What about the microdot?"

"We don't know, Tyson. When our backups stormed in, Jasco was searching Hank, who was unconscious and bleeding like hell. The shooter took off, then Jasco ran and was able to escape. Our people got a good look at him, though. The pen was still in Hank's pocket, but the microdot wasn't in it."

"That doesn't surprise me," Tyson said. "Hank Clarkson doesn't like pat deals. Too many people knew about the pen to suit him. He transferred the microdot to something else. Guaranteed."

"Yeah, and that's the problem," Ben said, sighing wearily. "We don't know where it is. Did Jasco get it? Or did Hank hide it so well that we didn't find it concealed on his body or in any of his personal property? We've just gotten a break, though."

"What do you mean?"

"Jasco managed to get into Chicago yesterday."

"Chicago? That's where Hank lives."

"And so does his daughter, Sophie. For Jasco to risk coming back into this country tells us that he's still after the microdot. We've lost him already. That man is so slippery it's a sin. Granted, he's crazy, certifiably insane, but a part of his mind operates like a well-tuned machine. Since word is out that Hank Clarkson is dead, we believe that Jasco is operating with the idea that Sophie Clarkson somehow obtained possession of the microdot. There's no other plausible reason for Jasco to go to Chicago."

"Hold it," Tyson said, raising one hand. "You've announced that Hank is dead?"

"Until we know where that microdot is, Tyson, it's the only way to totally protect Hank. Hospital security has been broken through before. Hank is too vulnerable under the circumstances. No one, I repeat, *no one*, other than a very select few are aware that Hank is alive.''

"What about his daughter? What about Sophie?"

"We told her that her father is dead."

"Ah, hell, Ben, that stinks, that really stinks."

"It was the only way to fully protect our agent. We shipped Sophie Clarkson a closed casket, said it was best left closed, and she complied. A funeral was held—it's done. You have forty-eight hours, MacDonald, to get some rest, then haul your butt to Chicago. Your assignment is to protect Sophie Clarkson from Jasco. She's covered now, but you'll take over. You are not—under any circumstances—to tell her that her father is alive. Clear?"

"Damn you, Wilson, I..."

"Is that clear?"

Tyson narrowed his eyes as he fought to regain control of his raging temper. He took a deep breath, then let it out slowly.

"Yeah," he said, fatigue evident in his voice, "it's clear."

"Good. That brings you up to date. You can go see Hank for five minutes."

Tyson spun on his heel and started toward the door.

"MacDonald."

Tyson stopped and glanced over one shoulder.

"Watch your back," Ben Wilson said quietly. "Jasco is nuts, which makes him that much more dangerous."

Tyson nodded, then left the room. Across the hall, his hands tightened on the rail edging the bed as his gaze swept over the beeping, gurgling machines that had tubes and wires leading to the unmoving figure in the bed.

"You sure picked a lousy place for a vacation, Hank," Tyson said, his voice raspy. His eyes lingered on the thick, white turban of gauze wrapped around Hank's head, then he looked at the pale, still face of his friend. "Come on, man, fight. Don't die on me, Hank. For God's sake, you can't just give up and die."

Tyson wished he could cry. He wanted to put his head down on the side of the bed and cry like a baby because Hank was hovering there between life and death. But he couldn't cry. He just didn't know how to release that kind of emotion, never had known how. All he could do for Hank was...

"Sophie," he said. "Don't worry about your daughter, Hank, because nothing is going to happen to her. I'm going to Chicago right now, and I'll make certain she's fine. You just concentrate on waking up, coming back from where you are. I'll take good care of your Sophie. I swear it."

Tyson stared at Hank for another long moment, then turned and walked out of the room.

Tyson didn't see Hank's right hand tremble, nor his thumb raise slightly in a valiant attempt to execute the age-old thumbs-up sign.

Then Hank Clarkson was still once more.

One

———

The wind whipped across the dark, deserted playground like a menacing beast seeking prey to tightly capture within its cold clutches.

Gritty sand was flung from the foot-high wooden enclosure that was long since devoid of paint. On a sunny day, the shallow box could entice a youngster to build imaginary towns, fairy-tale castles, bridges, dams and roads for matchbox cars. But on this blustery, bitterly cold night, the sand became stinging pellets mastered by the howling wind.

The rusty swings lurched back and forth at a frenzied pace, the old chains creaking in protest. As though propelled by phantom children, the swings seemed to be challenging each other to soar to daring heights.

Jasco stepped from behind one of the large trees edging the playground and stared at the elementary school adjacent to the play area. His hands were shoved into the pockets of the lightweight poplin jacket he wore, the collar turned up in a futile attempt to keep the cold at bay. His shoulders were hunched by unconscious instinct to try to keep warm by curling into his own body heat.

He wouldn't dare, he knew, ever approach a playground like this one in the light of day when children were there. The jagged, puckered scar that tracked his narrow face from his right eye to the edge of his mouth would frighten kids, cause them to scream in terror. The braver of the bunch might point at him, calling him taunting names, humiliate him as they performed for their laughing peers.

Children could be cruel, he thought, narrowing his eyes. Adults were cruel, too. Everyone, *everyone,* was mean and vicious. *Everyone.* But he'd finally had his revenge against the demon, the worst man of all—the one who had marked him years before and scarred his face with the sharp blade of a knife. Hank Clarkson, at long last, was dead.

Revenge, Jasco's mind echoed. *Sweet, so very sweet.* But there was one more step to be taken to complete his mission. One more...the elusive microdot.

He smiled in the darkness as he looked at the lighted windows on the first floor of the grimy, three-story brick school.

And then he laughed, throwing his head back as the humorless sound combined with the howling wind in a hideous, keening wail.

Sophie Clarkson pulled the front of her red cardigan sweater together, then folded her arms beneath her breasts as a shiver swept through her.

She glanced at the windows of the classroom and frowned as the glass rattled in the paint-chipped frames. The old-fashioned, ribbed radiator along the wall sputtered and hissed, banged, clanked and popped, producing little heat.

She redirected her attention to the twenty-one people of varying ages who had managed to maneuver their adult bodies into child-sized desks.

"As I was saying—" Sophie said, smiling "—as you have seen on your schedule that I gave you on the first night of class, we are midway through the eight-week course, and it's time to delve deeper into the subject of color.

"In interior design, color can be the deciding factor in whether a room has that undescribable *something* that takes one's breath away, or if it is merely mediocre. While I was in the process of obtaining my degree, I took two years of psychology. Those classes have been of immeasurable value to me in understanding the psychological effects of colors. So! On to color. The first example I want to show you is . . ."

Sophie stopped speaking as the door to the classroom opened. Twenty-one heads, plus Sophie's own, snapped around to see who was interrupting, an event that hadn't occurred during the previous three Thursday-night sessions.

A man entered and pulled the door closed behind him with a quiet click.

"May I help you?" Sophie asked.

Quite obviously he was in the wrong room, she mused. If ever there was a noncandidate for a free community course in interior design, this man was it. He had an—oh, what should she call it?—yes, an outdoorsy look about him. A raw ruggedness that seemed to be shouting the fact that he was all male and could not be tamed.

Fanciful thoughts, Sophie, she admonished herself, considering she'd never seen him before in her life. Of that fact she was positive. No red-blooded, breathing woman under eighty would ever forget having met this masculine specimen.

He was tall, dark and handsome—a TDH, to quote her business assistant and dearest friend, Janet. His features taken separately would not score well on the famous one-to-ten, she decided, as they were too rough edged, craggy, and his nose had a bump, either from genes or a well-placed right cross. But put all those features together, accentuated by the square jaw and high cheekbones, the tanned skin and thick, in-need-of-a-trim black hair, and this man was, quite simply...gorgeous.

"Sir?" Sophie said, smiling politely.

"I'll just take a seat in the back," he said. "Sorry to have interrupted your lecture."

Sophie frowned slightly as she watched him move to the rear of the room, absently noting that he'd spoken in a deep, rich voice. He had the rolling gait of an athlete...or maybe a cowboy, as evidenced by the sheepskin jacket he was now shrugging out of. What that man did for a black crewneck sweater and faded jeans was sinful.

"Miss Clarkson?" an elderly lady in one of the front desks said. "Colors?"

"Who?" Sophie said, then blinked. "Oh, yes, of course, colors. Do you have your pencils and notebooks ready? You'll want to jot down most of this to study later." Her gaze flickered to the back of the room, then her eyes collided with the man's dark brown eyes.

"You're more than welcome to sit down," she said.

He leaned one shoulder against the wall and crossed his arms loosely over his chest.

"I can't fit in that desk," he said. "This is fine. Carry on with your colors."

"I don't mean to be rude," Sophie said, cocking her head slightly to one side, "but are you certain this is where you want to be?"

"Positive," he said.

"Well," Sophie said, with a little shrug, "fine. I'm your instructor in interior design, Sophie Clarkson."

"MacDonald. Tyson MacDonald," he said, inclining his head. "Don't let me hold up your lecture on colors, Miss Clarkson," he added, smiling. "I'm sure it's very fascinating."

Oh-h-h, not fair, Sophie thought. All that, and a knock-'em-dead, flashing-white-teeth smile to boot.

Sophie nodded at him, and quickly held up a four-inch square of velvet. "Red. What do you immediately think of?"

"A bull," a teenage girl said. "A red flag in front of a bull."

"Blood," a man said.

As other suggestions were offered from the group, Tyson scrutinized Sophie.

So, this was Sophie Clarkson, he thought. Nice, very nice. Beautiful, actually. She was about five-six, had strawberry blond hair that fell in waves to her shoulders, and big blue eyes. Gray slacks covered legs that went from here to tomorrow, and a red cardigan over a white sweater didn't diminish the effect of her full breasts. Very, *very* nice.

The last picture Hank Clarkson had shown him, Tyson mused, had been an old, tattered snapshot showing Sophie as a gangly teenager with a mouthful of braces.

She was now twenty-seven and had done a superlative job of filling out. She had a degree in interior design and owned her business that had the whimsical name of Sophie's Attic. Single, she dated several different men, but in the past few months had been going out with Todd Lexington, an upwardly mobile, yuppie corporate attorney.

Sophie Clarkson. Hank's kid. Hank's baby girl, his pride and joy. Hank's Sophie, whom he'd raised with the help of a housekeeper after Mrs. Clarkson died of cancer when Sophie was three. Sophie, who now believed that she had no living relatives, no family, because she'd been told that Hank Clarkson was dead.

"Those are all interesting ideas as to what red represents," Sophie was saying, "and psychological studies have proven that red heightens—"

"Passion," Tyson said. "Arousal, sex appeal."

"I beg your pardon?" Sophie said, her eyes widening.

"I read it in a magazine," Tyson said. "Put red satin sheets on a bed and..."

"Mr. MacDonald," Sophie said, trying not to grind her teeth, "thank you for sharing your answer. However—" she shot him a quick but definite glare "—red has proven to be capable of increasing one's level of energy."

A grin broke across Tyson MacDonald's face.

"Therefore," Sophie said stiffly, managing to glower at him again, "it could be put to productive use in a room used for aerobics, gymnastics or any other physically exerting activity."

Tyson coughed loudly in an attempt to camouflage the burst of laughter that had escaped from deep in his chest.

"Mr. MacDonald," Sophie said, ever so very sweetly, "perhaps you could use a hefty dose of very cold water." She paused, smiled and batted her eyelashes just a tad for good measure. "There's a drinking fountain somewhere in the building, I'm sure."

"Score one point for you, Miss Clarkson," he said, smiling again. "Please, proceed."

"Thank you," she said, then added a very indignant sniff. "Red is fantastic for workout clothes themselves, such as sweatsuits, jogging shorts and tops. It also stimulates creativity, and is presently the accent color in more than one of the think tanks in Silicon Valley in California, where the mighty minds boggle their brains with computers."

A hand shot up.

"Yes, Mrs. Franklin?" Sophie said.

"If red increases energy and I used it in my kitchen, do you suppose my two teenagers would clean up quicker after their snacks?"

Sophie laughed. "Be careful with red in the kitchen. It also increases appetites."

A collective groan went up from the group as Sophie put down the red velvet square and picked up one of a medium shade of pink.

"I've decided we'll call this bubble-gum pink," she said.

And *he'd* call *her* fantastic, Tyson thought. She was quick, sharp as a tack. Oh, she'd inherited Hank's temper—there was no doubt about that—but she'd use it well. She'd be a handful for any man, and he had a feeling that a guy was never bored while in the company of Sophie. She knew her stuff, too, everything he'd ever wanted—or didn't want—to know about interior design.

"This shade of pink," Sophie said, "is soothing, evokes trust, has a calming effect. It's used with excellent results in detention centers for troubled teens. Though it sounds like a cliché to decorate a little girl's room in pink, she'll be happier for it, find a sense of contentment in her private haven. The tricky part is convincing a young boy to have his room done in pink."

The people in the class laughed, and eagerly awaited the next color swatch, taking copious notes as Sophie spoke. She went on to explain the psychological effects of both light and dark blue, as well as varying shades of yellow, green and violet. To Tyson's own amazement, he found himself listening to every word, discovering that the tremendous impact of color on the human brain *was* fascinating.

"In closing," Sophie said, "let me remind you that in using colors you have to overcome preconceived ideas, preprogrammed associations that have been in existence for a very long time.

"Black, for example, is considered somber, used to symbolize death, mourning..." She'd worn black to the funeral service for her father. Everyone there had been in black. He wouldn't have approved of that, not her dad, not vibrant, vital Hank Clarkson. "The Chinese wear white for mourning, while we Americans associate white with weddings. A red tablecloth used in a Chinese home says that the guest is held in high esteem, is very honored, and the list goes on from culture to culture."

Sophie paused for a moment, then continued, "But by knowing the subtle psychological effect of colors, you will accomplish exactly what you set out to do. That's it for tonight. Next week we'll delve into the world of antiques. Good night. I'll see you all next Thursday in this same cold, drafty room."

In a flurry of activity and chatter, the group gathered their belongings, collected coats from empty desks, bid

Sophie affectionate farewells, and each moved out the door.

Sophie lifted her briefcase from beneath the desk, snapped it open and began to place her notes and materials inside.

Tyson MacDonald, she knew, was still in the room. She could feel . . . somehow *feel* . . . his presence. She was absolutely, positively not going to look toward the rear of the room.

Yes, she was, she inwardly admitted.

She straightened from where she'd been slightly bent over next to the teacher's desk and turned to see Tyson take his jacket from the back of the small desk, then start slowly toward her.

The man was a hunter, a silent, soundless, stalking hunter, Sophie thought, unable to tear her gaze from his. A coiled, controlled readiness emanated from him, a predatory alertness that seemed to nearly crackle through the air with its intensity.

And those dark brown eyes, her mind rushed on. They were pinning her in place, making it difficult to breathe. Her heart beat in a wild cadence. Tyson MacDonald, was . . . was dangerous.

Tyson stopped directly in front of Sophie, leaving about two feet of space between them. Neither spoke for what seemed to be an eternity.

"Interesting lecture," Tyson said finally, breaking the silence. "You're an excellent teacher, and from what I hear, a very talented decorator."

"Thank you," Sophie said, hoping her voice was steadier than it had echoed in her own ears. "Well, class is dismissed. I must be going."

"Miss Clarkson," Tyson said, his voice very low, " . . . Sophie, if I may, I need to talk to you."

"You have a particular decorating problem, Mr. MacDonald? Why don't I give you one of my business cards, and you can phone me at work tomorrow?"

"It's Tyson, and no, I don't have a decorating problem. I really don't have anything to decorate."

"Then what . . ."

"It's about your father."

Sophie closed her eyes for a moment, struggling against tears that were never far from the surface. She opened her eyes, met Tyson's gaze again and lifted her chin.

"I'm sorry," she said. "It's only been just over a month since he . . . since he died. It has not been an easy time for me, and I still find it hard to believe that he's dead. But be that as it may, what is it that you wished to discuss with me about my father?"

"Could we get out of this place, go somewhere quiet, private?"

Sophie narrowed her eyes. "No, I don't think so, Mr. MacDonald."

Tyson stared up at the ceiling, shook his head, then looked at her again.

"I sure blew that, didn't I? No woman with half a brain would go off with a stranger in this section of Chicago."

"In *any* section of Chicago," she said. "We can talk here. No, the other instructors are leaving. I really must go. Why don't you come by my office tomorrow, Mr. MacDonald?"

"Tyson. Your office is in an old Victorian house that you restored nearly single-handedly. You live upstairs on the second floor. The main floor is devoted to Sophie's Attic. You donate your time every year to teach this class—free of charge. Hank Clarkson called you Soapy until you announced on your thirteenth birthday that you were all grown-up and should be called Sophie, befitting your status. The name Soapy came from the fact that as a toddler you couldn't quite pronounce Sophie, and it came out Soapy. Hank loved you more than life. I admired and respected him more than any man I've ever known.''

"I see," Sophie said, looking at Tyson intensely. "I...yes..." She stopped speaking, then nodded slowly. "Of course, it all makes sense now. The way you move, the tight, controlled command of your body, the means by which you found out so much about me, including where I would be tonight. You're one of them. Well? Whip out the slim leather case, Mr. MacDonald, that says you're with the State Department. But we know, don't we, that it's much more complicated than that. You're in a special, secret agency, which our government would never publicly acknowledge. You go places, and do things, known only to a precious few. Oh, yes, you're definitely one of them.''

"Sophie..."

"And so was my father. I loved him unconditionally, but I have no wish to speak with anyone else from that damn agency.''

Suddenly, a muscle ticked in Tyson's tightly clenched jaw.

"Granted," Sophie continued, "my father obviously was fond of you to have shared our family stories, telling you about my nickname being Soapy and...'' Sudden tears filled her eyes. "I miss him. God, how I miss him. He was away so much when I was growing up, yet it was all right because he always came home. *He always came home.* I'm twenty-seven years old, a supposedly mature, sophisticated career woman but, damn it, I don't know how to handle the raw, stark truth that he's *never* coming home again."

But that *wasn't* the truth, Tyson's mind hammered. Hank isn't dead. He's fighting for his life, hanging on, and he might yet come home to Sophie again. Lord, what the agency was doing to Sophie was cruel. He hated—really hated—this lie.

Sophie shook her head in self-disgust and dashed the tears from her cheeks.

"I'm sorry for falling apart like this," she said. "It was inexcusable."

"It was real," Tyson said. "A daughter who is grieving for a beloved father. Hank is . . . was . . . a lucky man, and he knew it."

"Thank you for that," Sophie said, turning to snap her briefcase closed. "Now if you'll excuse me, I don't believe we have anything further to talk about. I have no desire to sit in front of a cozy fire hearing you reminisce about the good old days with Hank Clarkson in God only knows what desolate spots of the world, and how many people you had to kill to complete your assignments. In my opinion, that just doesn't add up to a fun evening."

"Lord, you're a hypocrite," Tyson said none too quietly. "One minute you're all tears and fond memories of dear old Dad, and the next you're talking about him and anyone who worked with him or believed in the same things he did, as though they're scums. How can you do that? Just switch emotional channels about your own father?"

Sophie snatched her briefcase from the desk, then lifted her coat and purse from the chair behind it. She turned halfway to look at Tyson.

She was still unnaturally pale, Tyson noted, but her eyes no longer shimmered with tears, making them appear like glimmering sapphires.

"I have no intention of explaining anything to you," Sophie said. "You came here, apparently to express your condolences regarding my father's death, and I accept your sentiments. We have nothing more to say to each other, Mr. MacDonald. Good night."

She started across the room at a brisk pace.

"Damn it," Tyson said fiercely under his breath. He covered the distance between them in long strides, his hand shooting out to grip Sophie's arm. "Would you hold it a minute?"

Sophie stopped and looked at him, at his hand where it held her arm, then at his face again. The fury building within her showed itself in bright flashes of pink on her cheeks.

"Okay, okay," Tyson said, jerking his hand from her arm. "Now your eyes are laser beams and I'm a dead man. Would you cool off for a second and think? While we've been standing here declaring war, the other teachers and all the students are probably long gone. Are you really going out into a dark parking lot alone in this neighborhood?"

Sophie blinked. "Oh."

"Yeah…oh," he said, shrugging into his jacket. "I'll walk you to your car, then follow you home."

"I would appreciate your escorting me to my vehicle, Mr. MacDonald," Sophie said. "However, it won't be necessary to drive the distance between here and my residence."

"Lord, you can really talk snooty when you put your mind to it, can't you?" He shook his head. "Let's go." He started toward the door.

"You are the rudest, most arrogant—"

"I've heard them all," he interrupted. "We're leaving the room now, Miss In-Your-High-And-Mighty Mode. Then we'll exit the building. I'll walk you to your car, you'll get in, lock the doors. I'll drive my car, and meet you at your house. Then..."

"No."

"Then if you don't let me inside your house so that I can talk to you..."

"No."

"I'll break down the damn door!" he yelled.

Sophie jerked in shock at Tyson's sudden and *very* loud outburst.

"Oh," was all she managed to say.

"I'm glad we understand the program," he said. He opened the classroom door, stepped back and bowed. "After you, ma'am."

"Sir?" Sophie said as she moved past him.

"Yes?"

"Shut up!" she shrieked, then stomped down the hall.

Tyson shook his head again and started after her. To his own surprise, he chuckled in the next instant.

Two

As Tyson followed Sophie through the heavy traffic, he decided that her choice of automobile fitted her perfectly. It was a compact car, which would be economical to drive, easy to maneuver in the always-surging Chicago traffic, and could be zipped into a parking place much too small for a big gas-guzzler.

But, he thought, a reluctant smile tugging at the corners of his mouth, let it not be said that Sophie Clarkson was one hundred percent practical. The little car was candy-apple red. Bright red. Catch-me red, as the cops called it. And Sophie drove just above the speed limit, treating yellow lights as though they were as green as spring grass.

Oh, yes, she was something. And he couldn't help but wonder what it would be like to make love with Sophie Clarkson, to have that passion stroked not by rage or sadness but by desire, directed totally toward him.

Tyson shifted on the seat, and his grip on the steering wheel tightened. He felt his body react to the image in his mind's eye of Sophie reaching up her arms to welcome him into her bed, her hair an enticing tangle on the pillow.

Those lush, long legs would wrap around him like a satiny smooth cage trapping him in a prison he'd have no wish to escape from. She'd match the pounding rhythm of his body with that of her own, and they would be flung up and over the abyss as they reached the height of their climb. They'd...

"MacDonald, stow it," he said, then added a few well-chosen expletives.

Heat coiled low in his body, and his manhood ached for release. He was fantasizing like a young teenager about a woman, and was thoroughly disgusted with himself. And as if that wasn't bad enough, the woman was the daughter of a man who was everything and more a friend could ever be to Tyson.

As Tyson pulled in behind Sophie in her driveway, he was back under control. He had simply fallen prey to the fact that he'd been too long without a woman, but he would be strictly business now. He was there for a very definite purpose—a mission—and he had every intention of seeing it through to its proper end.

A stairway had been constructed at the side of the house, allowing Sophie to come and go without having to enter the business area below if she chose not to.

She ignored Tyson as she went up the stairs and unlocked the door. She knew that he'd make good on his threat to break the door down if she closed it in his face. But while she'd reluctantly accepted the realization that he was going to come into her home, she felt no compulsion to make him feel welcome.

When they entered the living room, Sophie turned on several lights, placed her briefcase and purse on the shelf of the front closet and hung up her coat. Tyson removed his jacket and draped it rather haphazardly over the back of a chair.

"This is a sharp place," he said, nodding in approval. "It's in a good section of town, very classy, but I noticed that most of the homes in the past few blocks are actually businesses."

"The area was rezoned," Sophie said, standing across the room from him. She should, she supposed, ask him to sit down, but decided not to. "Mr. MacDonald, what was it that you wished to discuss with me?"

"It's Tyson," he said absently as he continued to survey the room. "You must have knocked out some walls to make this area so large. Did you have to add the kitchen? Well, yeah, you would have had to because there were only bedrooms and baths up here, right? Clever, very innovative. Let's see now . . . white wicker furniture with mauve and pale blue as your . . . accent colors. Yeah, accent colors. The shades you've chosen evoke calmness, relieve stress and enhance creativity."

"You were actually paying attention to my lecture tonight?"

"Sure. You made it very interesting. I found myself enjoying it."

Sophie shook her head. "You're a walking contradiction, Mr. MacDonald. I would have bet that you were bored out of your mind."

"Sophie, do you think you could relax a bit and call me Tyson? This 'Mr. MacDonald' stuff is making me feel like an extremely old man and I'm only thirty-six. It's Tyson, okay?"

"Well, I, yes, all right... Tyson. May we get on with the subject at hand?"

He crossed the room and sank onto the puffy cushions of the sofa.

"Don't you want to sit down?" he said.

"How kind of you to offer," Sophie said dryly.

Instead of sitting down, though, she first went to the fireplace and set a match to the kindling and logs in the hearth, then replaced the screen. She went over to a fan-backed wicker chair. The moment that she sat down, she slipped off her shoes.

Tyson leaned forward, resting his elbows on his knees and laced his fingers loosely together. He looked at Sophie for a long moment before he spoke.

"Sophie," he said finally, "I've been informed that when the government officials came to you to tell you that Hank... that Hank was dead, you didn't press for details. They said he had been killed while on official government business, and that was that."

"There was no point in my asking questions I knew they wouldn't answer. My father warned me years ago that if something happened to him that I should simply accept it and not expect to ever know the complete truth of the matter."

Tyson nodded. "He was right. They'll volunteer nothing and lie through their teeth if pressure is applied."

"Charming people," Sophie said dryly.

"The State Department has forwarded Hank's personal possessions to you, haven't they?"

"Yes. Mr.... Tyson, why are we having this conversation? The death of my father has been difficult for me, *very* difficult. It might have helped, a little at least, if I could have seen him and said a proper goodbye. But the casket was closed, and I was instructed to leave it as it was. That led to my imagining the worst possible scenarios about how my father died. I—'' She closed her eyes for a moment to regain control of her emotions, then looked at him again. ''Why are you doing this to me? It's cruel.''

''I have no choice. The assignment that Hank was on isn't finished. There are loose ends, dangerous loose ends, that directly involve you.''

''What do you mean?''

Tyson got to his feet, a deep frown on his face as he dragged one restless hand through his hair.

''There's a top-security microdot missing, Sophie. Did Hank ever mention a man named Jasco?''

''No, my dad never used the names of anyone involved in his work. Who is Jasco?''

''A lunatic. A man who is truly insane. He was waiting to ambush Hank the night of the transfer of the microdot. Jasco has hated Hank Clarkson for many years because, well, because of something that happened between them a long time ago. Jasco had been in prison, thanks to Hank, got out a year ago and disappeared. He surfaced that night in the alley in... it's really not important where it all took place.''

Sophie's eyes widened. ''Are you saying that this Jasco killed my father? You know who did it?''

Tyson nodded. ''Jasco didn't actually pull the trigger on the gun, but it was his show. He uses a knife, has never carried a gun as far we know. There was a shooter with him, who followed Jasco's orders and shot Hank.''

''Dear Lord,'' Sophie whispered.

''I realize this isn't easy to listen to, Sophie, but I have to tell you the facts.''

''God, it's so stark, cold, so...'' She shook her head.

"In the confusion that night," Tyson went on, "the transfer of the microdot got fouled up. The thing is, we didn't know where it ended up. We still don't, actually. But we've discovered that Jasco obviously doesn't have it, because he's taking big risks to find it."

"Tyson, you said that I was directly involved in this thing. Just what exactly did you mean by that?"

"Jasco is in Chicago, and there's only one reason for him to be here. He's convinced that somehow *you* obtained possession of the microdot. He's come to get it, Sophie. He will do whatever he feels is necessary to achieve that end. Your life is in danger. Jasco won't hesitate to kill you to get what he wants."

"I don't have a microdot," she said, her voice rising. "For God's sake, Tyson, are you listening to what you're saying to me? The man who killed my father is now prepared to murder me to get something I know nothing about. This is crazy, totally bizarre!"

"I know, and I'm sorry there isn't a better way to present this to you," he said quietly, "but, unfortunately, that's the way it stacks up."

"No," she said. "No. I'm still trying to deal with the fact that my father is dead. Now I'm supposed to say, 'Well, isn't this fascinating? The killer is coming after *me* for round two.' It's too much, it's..." She shook her head as her lips formed a silent *no*.

As Tyson's shocking and horrifying words continued to echo in Sophie's mind and beat unmercifully against her brain, emotions surged through her like a rushing river out of control.

She felt suddenly disoriented, off kilter, as though she had been flung into a dark pit and was viewing Tyson through the wrong end of a telescope. He seemed far, far away, and she could no longer hear his taunting words that had continued to repeat over and over like an insistent, sadistic drummer.

A rushing noise in her ears was accompanied by black dots flashing before her eyes. The room, she thought hazily, was tilting, tilting, and she'd slip from the edge and…disappear forever…disappear like her father and, *Oh, dear God, no!*

The next sensation that Sophie registered was of something tight gripping the back of her head. She was moving down and the floor was coming up.

"That's it, Sophie," Tyson said, "we're putting your head between your knees. Take even breaths, not too deep, not too shallow. Easy does it."

Sophie blinked and took a breath, dispelling the last of the fog from her mind. She was, she realized, bent over like a pretzel, staring at the carpeting on the floor. Tyson's hand was on the back of her head, and his arm was across her chest, tucked snugly next to her breasts,

It was such a nice strong arm, she mused, so very masculine, and Tyson smelled good, like soap and fresh air. And if she kept blithering in her mind, she could postpone having to square off against what he had said, not face it head-on. She'd just stay where she was for the next five years or so, nearly standing on her nose with Tyson's marvelous arm cradling her breasts.

"Okay?" Tyson said, snapping Sophie out of her rambling thoughts. He slowly withdrew his arm, then lifted his hand from her head. "Now, sit up slowly, just ease your way upward."

Sophie did as instructed, then leaned her head back on the chair and closed her eyes.

"Good," Tyson said. "You have color in your face. You turned the shade of bleached flour, and you were about to go out on me. I'm sorry, Sophie. There was no way to inch around what I said. All I could do was...well, just say it.''

Sophie opened her eyes and looked at him. ''So, you're here on an official assignment. I assume you're here to protect me, or some such thing, from that maniac who is out there somewhere, capture him and find the precious microdot. This is like living in a bad movie.''

Tyson sank back onto the sofa. ''My first priority is your safety. As for the rest of it, I'll call the shots as they come up. I have men assigned to me who are ready to follow my orders to the letter. To get to you, Sophie, Jasco is going to have to go through me—and he won't find it that easy to do.''

''You'd risk your life for me?''

''Yes.''

''Why, Tyson?''

''Sophie, Hank Clarkson is...was...the best friend I've ever had. I worked with him on many occasions over the past ten years. He taught me more than I can begin to tell you. He saved my life three times when I was green and reckless early on.''

Tyson stopped speaking and turned his head to stare into the leaping orange flames of the fire in the hearth.

''I owe him, Sophie. I owe Hank a helluva lot. He's not here to protect you from Jasco, but I am. Nothing, *nothing,* is going to happen to you.''

A shiver coursed through Sophie as she heard the steely edge to Tyson's voice, saw the cold glint in the brown depths of his eyes.

This was the dark side of Tyson MacDonald she was witnessing. This had been a part of her father she had never seen but that he'd told her was there. She had learned over the years how to deal with the knowledge, the harsh truth of what her father did when he left her.

But she had never seen in Hank Clarkson, not once, what she now saw in Tyson MacDonald. And God help her, she was inwardly cheering that it was there.

"Sophie?"

"Yes," she whispered, "I understand. You'll do everything possible to keep me out of harm's way. But I want more. I want Jasco to pay for the death of my father. Find Jasco, Tyson. Please? Oh, God, my father, my father is dead." She covered her face with her hands.

"Oh, man," he said, lunging to his feet.

He crossed to where Sophie sat and stopped in front of her, searching his mind for something, hopefully the right thing, to say.

He was out of his element; he knew it, and felt a knot of frustration in his gut as he acknowledged the fact. He was a loner, and it had always suited him just fine. Hank Clarkson had been the only one ever allowed beyond Tyson's solid shield that kept people at bay.

Women found him intriguing for reasons only they might be able to explain, and he could pick and choose from those available. He made no promises, no false declarations of commitment or love. He was a challenge, he supposed, to women. A trophy they wanted to boast about because he gave the impression he just didn't need them, could take 'em or leave 'em.

But right now, he inwardly fumed. Right this damn minute, he wished he knew how to comfort a woman, sooth her, be able to speak the words that flowed so easily from those more socially adept than he.

Sophie was crying. The soft sobs he could hear were tearing through him like the blade of a knife.

"Ah, Sophie," he said. He hesitated only a second longer, then gripped her upper arms and gently drew her to her feet.

Sophie wrapped her arms around Tyson's waist, buried her face in the soft material of his sweater and wept.

He encircled her back with one arm and pulled her tightly to him, his free hand tenderly stroking her head as racking sobs swept through her body. He tipped his head down to lay his cheek against the top of her silken hair. And held her. He simply held her, and Sophie cried as though the tears were coming from the very depths of her soul.

They were sorrowful yet cleansing tears. For Tyson they were the tears that he, himself, had not been able to shed, the tears that had caught in his throat and burned in his chest but wouldn't flow free, not even for Hank. It was as though Sophie was crying for both of them.

The fire in the hearth crackled, the warming flames casting a golden glow over the pair. Time lost meaning.

Tyson felt the heat begin to build deep within him, coil, churn, tighten. Sophie was nestled close to his body, her breasts pressing against his chest as she clung to him. He was acutely aware of her fresh, feminine aroma that assaulted him with every breath he took.

He had offered her comfort from her pain, he thought in self-disgust, and he was reacting to her on a plane of man and woman—a very desirable woman.

What was haunting him was the knowledge that he had the power to ease her grief and sorrow, to halt the tears that were racking her slender body. All he had to say was "Hank is alive."

But he couldn't do it.

Even if he swore her to secrecy, it was too risky. Jasco's twisted mind was strangely astute in some areas of reasoning, while wildly irrational in others. If Jasco sensed, saw, any change in Sophie, any clue that Sophie was suddenly not as distraught as she had been, she would be in even greater danger.

No, he had to keep silent.

As Sophie's tears began to ebb, she made no attempt to draw back from the heat and solid strength of Tyson's body. His arm that crossed her back didn't feel oppressive, but seemed instead to represent a barrier between her and the unsettling world beyond, a circle of safety she was in no rush to be free of.

She was conscious of the steady beat of his heart, drawing solace from knowing that after this beat would come another, then another, because Tyson was alive, and real, and earthy and sensual, and reaffirmed life over death.

So many tears she had cried since receiving the bone-chilling news that her father would never again come home. But none of those tears shed had been like those of this night. These had come from a place deep within her, which she hadn't even known existed. In their wake had crept peace, tentatively at first, then growing stronger, like a bright beacon on a foggy night.

She would now be able to smile at the special, cherished memories of times spent with her father, look at old photos, replay scenarios in her mind for the sheer pleasure of it. She would gather her courage to go on with her existence and, as she traveled that road alone, without Hank, she would do whatever was necessary to bring to justice the evil creature who had stolen his life.

Sophie stirred in Tyson's embrace and felt his hand leave her head. A moment later, a clean white handkerchief appeared in front of her eyes.

She took the handkerchief in one hand, then slowly moved backward and away from the solid, warm comfort of Tyson's body. She swept the tears from her cheeks with the soft cloth, dabbed at her nose, then drew a wobbly breath that was expelled with a sigh. She met Tyson's gaze.

"Thank you," she said. "It's an awful cliché, but I needed that. I've cried so much in the past two weeks. There were so many emotions to deal with—anger, self-pity. And the question of why? Why? Why? There was no one, not even my closest friends, who I could talk to because they didn't know what my father actually did for a living. But you *do* know. You cared about him, and these tears tonight were for Hank, pure and simple. Thank you, Tyson MacDonald. You're a very patient, very understanding man."

"No," he said, shaking his head. "I'm really not but, well, I'm glad I could help." He paused. "Sophie, would you like me to leave for now? You're obviously all worn-out. Maybe it would be best if we spoke tomorrow about... Well, what I've said to you has been quite a shock, and you haven't even had time to fully recover from the initial news of Hank's death. So, for tonight, why don't we put this on hold and you can get some sleep?"

"No, I won't be able to sleep until I somehow relax, unwind, at least a little. Please, let's sit down. Would you like something to drink?"

"No, thanks." He sat on the sofa, and Sophie sank onto the fan-backed chair. He stretched his arms along the top of the sofa, and a frown knitted his brows as he looked at her. "Hank told you early on about what he really did for a living, didn't he?"

"Yes, and I realized that he would have been in trouble with his superiors if they'd known he'd told me. He sat me down when I was sixteen and said it was time I knew the truth. He also stressed that it was imperative that I never tell anyone else.''

"You had a rare and special relationship.''

"Yes. We were separated a great deal of the time, but it made us appreciate what we had even more. I have wonderful memories of things shared with my dad.''

Tyson nodded, and they were silent for several minutes, each lost in their own thoughts.

"Sophie,'' Tyson finally said, "would you mind if I looked at Hank's possessions that were sent to you by the State Department?''

"Of course you can see them, but there wasn't much. He didn't carry a lot, Tyson, none of you do. There wasn't even a driver's license in his wallet.'' Sophie started to rise, then stopped, a rather questioning expression on her face. "I'll show you what I received, Tyson, but why the interest in the odds and ends from my father's pockets?''

"I can't leave any stone unturned, that's all. I realize those items have been thoroughly examined for the microdot by the powers that be, but I'd just feel better knowing I'd looked them all over, too. Humor me. There's no concrete reason for me to be doing this.''

"I see,'' Sophie said, nodding. She got to her feet, crossed the room and pulled open the center drawer of a desk that sat against the far wall. She removed a large beige envelope and retraced her steps. "Here you are.''

"Thank you,'' Tyson said, taking it from her. Lord, she was beautiful.... And he'd sure as hell better remember his resolve to stick to business. "Well, here goes.''

Sophie wrapped her hands around her elbows as Tyson opened the envelope and slid the contents onto the sofa cushion next to him. The excruciating pain she'd experienced when she'd first seen those few items was dulled, she realized. It didn't cut through her with an agonizing, sharp edge.

Because of the tears she had shed while held in Tyson's strong arms, Sophie knew she had now begun the process of recovering from her loss, was regaining at least a modicum of control over her emotions.

She would always and forever miss her father, but now she could dwell on his memory if she chose to without falling apart. She was going to be all right.

"Inexpensive watch," Tyson said, placing it back in the envelope. "That thing never wore out or got broken. Hank had that watch for as long as I can remember. Jackknife. Key chain with no keys. Wallet. That's it?"

"Yes, that's all that there was. I made that key chain for him when I was a Brownie. I was seven or eight, I guess. I tooled the flower on the little strip of leather. One of the fathers drilled holes in nickels so we could attach them for decoration. I think that's illegal, actually—defacing coins like that. The whole thing is worse for wear, but I've decided that I'll use it for my keys now. I hadn't seen that tiny gold charm hanging next to the nickel, but it has obviously been there awhile, as it's scratched and dented."

Tyson picked up the key chain. "I've seen this in the past, but not for a long time. I don't recall if I ever noticed the gold charm before. It's a ballerina, I think. Yeah, it's a dancer."

"He must have seen it somewhere, and it struck his fancy," Sophie said. "My father told me he'd always carry the key chain, but I didn't actually see it often. He never put any keys on it, that I do know."

"You're right. If he'd had personal keys attached to it, he would have had to leave it behind when he went on an assignment. He considered this a good-luck charm rather than a key chain. You don't mind if I look through the wallet, do you?''

''No, go right ahead.'' She sat down on the chair, then watched Tyson methodically search the worn leather wallet.

When he was finished, he put the wallet and other items back into the envelope.

''Damn,'' he said. ''Nothing. Twenty-two dollars in the wallet, and a coupon that expired six months ago. That's it.''

''Yes, I know,'' Sophie said wearily. ''I still have to sort through everything at his house. I just haven't had the emotional fortitude to do it yet. I grew up in that home, and I'm not sure what to do with it. I'd hate to sell it, but the idea of being a landlady if I rented it out doesn't appeal to me, either. Oh, never mind, that's my problem to solve, not yours.''

''Sophie,'' Tyson said, ''I have to ask you something. You obviously loved your father very much, but just as obvious is your disapproval of what he did for a living. That came across loud and clear when you referred to me as 'one of them.' You have intense negative feelings about your dad's occupation, yet your love for Hank was very strong. Hell, I can't get this across.''

''I know what you're saying, Tyson. It's as though I have contradicting reactions to the same man. Over the years, I learned to separate my father from his work. I saw Hank Clarkson as a wonderful, warm, loving father, who thought the sun rose and set just for me. I stopped right there. I didn't acknowledge that he was capable of killing another human being in cold blood, could lie, cheat, deceive, do whatever was necessary to achieve his goal. That part of him made him one of them, just as you are, and I ignored it for the most part. Childish? Maybe, but it worked for me, and didn't tarnish my relationship with Hank.''

''I see,'' Tyson said. ''That makes sense, I suppose. That leaves me firmly planted in the arena of 'one of them.' Right?''

Sophie looked at him for a long moment. ''Yes,'' she finally said quietly, ''I guess it does.'' But it had been Tyson who had held her, comforted her while she cried the tears she'd needed to shed. It was Tyson who was now prepared to stand between her and the insanity of Jasco, to protect her at the risk of his own life. It was Tyson who... No, now stop it. Tyson MacDonald was one of them. ''Yes.''

Tyson nodded as a muscle ticked in his tightly clenched jaw.

''Well, that's clear enough,'' he said.

And for some unknown reason, it wasn't setting well with him, he realized. Sophie had labeled him, stuck him in a slot, and that was that. Damn it, he was doing an important job for his country—just as Hank had. But while she'd separated Hank the agent from Hank the father, Tyson MacDonald was to be nothing more than a single entity called ''one of them.'' Fine, if that was how she wanted it. It was no big deal to him. But why did he have a knot in his gut the size of a bowling ball?

''Well,'' he said, getting to his feet, ''that's it for tonight. I hope you'll be able to sleep, Sophie. There will be agents watching this place twenty-four hours a day, so you needn't worry.''

''Right,'' she said dryly. ''I won't give any of this a second thought. After all, what's the fuss about? There's only a maniac on the loose out there who murdered my

father. This insane man, Jasco, thinks I have a microdot
I know nothing about, and he won't hesitate to kill me to
get it. That scenario, Mr. MacDonald, does not make for
sweet, peaceful dreams.''

Three

Sophie's Attic was charming and cozy, yet contained enough space to be very efficiently run.

The kitchen provided the means to serve tea to clients, as well as making it possible for Sophie and her assistant, Janet Smith, to prepare their lunches. The bedrooms held endless sample books of wallpaper, fabric and carpeting. There were always items on hand waiting to be put in place in a client's newly decorated area. It wasn't unusual to have an old-fashioned spinning wheel sitting next to an ultramodern glass-and-chrome table in one of the bedrooms.

Sophie's office was tucked into the corner of one of the rooms, as well. The desk was a jumbled mess, but off-limits to everyone but herself, as she claimed to know exactly what everything was for.

The living room was arranged to give a combined aura of comfort and class, with a crackling fire in the hearth during the cold months in Chicago. There, Sophie would sit with a client, sipping tea, showing samples of colors and fabrics, discussing the multitude of details that had to be tended to in interior design.

The stairs at the side of the entryway had a red velvet rope across the bottom to silently state that no one was to go beyond the barrier. The stairs allowed Sophie to leave her living area above and arrive at work below if she chose not to use the outside staircase she'd had built onto the house.

The morning after Tyson MacDonald's emergence into Sophie's life, she walked slowly down the interior stairs. She was tired before the workday had even begun. She hadn't slept well at all, had tossed and turned, and nightmares had plagued her when she did finally doze.

Sophie unhooked the velvet rope, stepped beyond it, then put it back in place. After unlocking the front door and turning the sign to Open, she started a fire in the fireplace. Snow flurries were beginning to fall outside, and the warming flames looked especially inviting. With her hands wrapped around her elbows, she stared into the nearly hypnotizing fire, her mind echoing every word that Tyson had said the previous night.

Dear heaven, she thought, things like this didn't happen to ordinary citizens, people who obeyed the law and worked hard at their chosen profession. But then, Hank Clarkson hadn't been an ordinary citizen.

And neither was Tyson MacDonald.

Sophie sighed. Tyson was one of *them*. She'd witnessed the cold, dark side of him.

But Tyson MacDonald was also capable of tenderness, understanding, giving comfort without standing in judgment of tears shed. And Tyson was capable of making her more aware of her own femininity than ever before.

A shiver coursed through Sophie, and she knew it was caused by more than fear of what he had told her. It also stemmed from the remembrance of being held so tightly in Tyson's strong arms, nestled against the hard contours of his body, inhaling his aroma and feeling the heated stirrings of desire deep within her.

Damn that man, Sophie fumed. She didn't want to be told that her life was in danger. And she *did not* want to be drawn like a metal sliver by the incredible masculine magnetism of Tyson.

The sound of the tinkling bells above the front door brought Sophie from her reverie, and she turned to see Janet entering the room.

Janet Smith was an extremely talented interior decorator. She looked younger than her twenty-four years. She was five feet tall, plump to the point that she'd never miss twenty pounds and had short, fuzzy, mousy brown hair that fell victim to her penchant for trying out home permanents. She was fun and funny, had a smile always at the ready and was Sophie's best friend.

"Oh, mercy me, it's cold out there," Janet said.

"Take off your coat and come by the fire."

"I definitely will. My toes and fingers are icicles. But take these first. Some lazy delivery boy, I presume, dumped these on the porch. You'd think he could have rung the bell, wouldn't you? This poor, frozen flower doesn't look too healthy. I don't see a card, but a buck says these gifts aren't from your Todd Lexington. That guy doesn't have a romantic bone in his body." She crossed the room to where Sophie stood by the fireplace.

Sophie frowned as she accepted the single flower that was wrapped in green tissue and a small, flat square

package covered in the same type of paper. Janet removed her coat, went to hang it up and returned to find
Sophie still frowning at the two items.

"You haven't opened the package?" Janet said.
"Here, give me that defrosting flower, and let's see what
the other goody is."

"Yes, all right," Sophie said, handing Janet the tissue-wrapped flower. Sophie tore off the paper to reveal
a book with pictures of flowers on the paper dustcover.
The book was titled *Dictionary of Flowers*. "There's
nothing written inside saying who it's from," she said,
flipping through the pages.

"Oh, a secret admirer," Janet said, beaming. "How
exciting, how wonderful, how—" she frowned "—frus-
trating. This will drive me crazy until we find out who
sent you this stuff. Hey, wait a minute. Maybe it's a
game, you know what I mean? Clues, we have clues.
Look up this flower in that dictionary."

"Oh, I see what you're getting at," Sophie said, nodding. "That's a rhododendron, isn't it? Yes, here's a
picture of one and..." Her voice trailed off, and her eyes
widened as she stared at the book.

"Sophie?" Janet said. "What's wrong? What does the
dictionary say about rhododendrons?"

"They deliver the message of danger," she said, her
voice unsteady. "That's what it says here." She looked at
Janet's startled expression, then tried desperately to find
words of reason to calm the younger woman.

"This is someone's idea of a joke," Janet said.
"Right? Right. Of course it is. What other explanation
could there be? Who do you know who has this kind of
an offbeat sense of humor?"

It's not a joke, Sophie's mind screamed. This was a
message, a warning, from Jasco. Tyson was right. Jasco

had a sick and twisted mind. Dear Lord, it was all so frightening.

"Sophie?" Janet said. "Why are you so pale? Why do you look scared out of your socks? Why aren't you telling me whose sense of humor matches this less-than-wonderful nonsense?"

"Janet, get serious, will you? Of course this is a joke. Why, I can think of six people right off the top of my head who would consider this hysterically funny."

Janet narrowed her eyes. "Name one."

"Name one. Name one? Well, sure, um..." The front door of the house opened to the accompaniment of the tinkling bells. Sophie's head snapped around, and her eyes widened for a moment before a smile of relief lit up her face. "Tyson MacDonald. See, Janet? He even appears at the scene of the crime to enjoy my reaction. Cute joke, Tyson. You momentarily scared the bejeebers out of both Janet and me."

"I did, huh?" he said, smiling. "Well, score one for me." His gaze flickered quickly over the book in Sophie's hand, the flower in Janet's. "Extremely clever, don't you think?"

"To send a rhododendron that the dictionary says stands for danger?" Sophie said. "Oh, yes, very clever, you sneaky beast."

Nicely done, Sophie Clarkson, Tyson thought. She was definitely Hank's kid—quick, sharp, had managed to fill him in on what was going on without further alarming the other woman standing there.

"Oh, Janet, this is Tyson MacDonald. Tyson, my assistant, Janet Smith."

"A living, breathing TDH...that's tall, dark and handsome," Janet said cheerfully. "Goodness, you're gorgeous, Tyson MacDonald. Where did Sophie find you?''

"In school," Tyson said pleasantly. "You know, that class Sophie's teaching about the color red increasing the intensity of passion?"

"That does it," Sophie said. She took the flower from Janet. "Janet, Mrs. Jameson will be here soon to see the fabric swatches for her bedroom. Would you please make certain the presentation is ready for her review?"

"Okay," Janet said. "While I'm doing that, I'll decide if I'm going to forgive you for not telling me you found a TDH running around loose. Bye for now, Tyson MacDonald. It was great to meet you." She waggled the fingers of one hand in the air as she left the room.

Tyson watched Janet until she disappeared, then he nodded. "I like her."

"She's marvelous," Sophie said, setting the flower and book on an end table, "*and* my closest friend."

Tyson's gaze switched from the doorway to Sophie. "Closest friend? You said you had no one to really talk to about Hank. Is Janet the exception to that? Does she know the truth about your father's occupation?"

Sophie sighed. "No. Janet and I met in college. She was a couple of years behind me, but we kept in constant touch after I graduated. When I started the renovations on this house four years ago, she showed up unannounced with her three brothers, and they all pitched in to help."

"Nice," Tyson said, nodding.

"Janet walked away from a well-paying, secure position with a prestigious firm to take a chance on me and Sophie's Attic. She was right there by my side the minute I called and told her that my father had died. Believe me, Tyson, I've wanted to share the truth with her. At times when Hank was away, it was a heavy weight on my mind. But I gave my father my solemn promise that I would never divulge his secret, and I never have.''

"I should have realized that without asking," he said. "You're Hank's daughter. That in itself would have provided me with the answer to the question."

"Thank you," she said. "To say I'm Hank's daughter in that manner is a lovely compliment." She paused. "You know, Tyson, before last night, before I cried the way I did, I would have been pushed over an emotional edge and wept because of what you just said. Now? I can treasure the gift of your compliment, as well as the image of my dad your words evoke in my mental vision. I'm very grateful to you for your kindness last evening."

Kindness? Tyson thought. What would Sophie think if she knew that desire, passion, had been on the scene, as well—right up there in bold print with what she was labeling kindness?

"Yeah, well," he said, deciding a change of subject was called for. "Let's get down to business, shall we? You did some impressive, fancy verbal footwork with Janet about this ugly flower. Was there anything to indicate which florist it came from? Or if it even was purchased at a flower shop?"

"No, there's no card, no writing in the book, nothing. I'd say it was bought at a florist because this tissue is shiny, coated differently than gift-wrap tissue. He may have asked for an extra piece to wrap the book in." She hesitated. "Tyson, this is Jasco's doing, isn't it?"

Tyson nodded, his expression grim. "I'd bet the farm on it. Before I came in here, I checked with my man who's on duty outside. He said a plain panel truck pulled up earlier, and a fat, elderly guy carried a tissue-wrapped flower to the door. It would seem that Jasco has broadened his scope into the world of disguises. He knows he was recognized in that alley when Hank was shot, and he's reducing the risk factor for himself. Damn, this is going to make things even more difficult.''

''Tyson, why did he do this? If he's after the micro-dot, why jeopardize that goal by appearing, disguise or not, in plain view for a purpose not related whatsoever to the microdot? There's no logic there as far as I can see.''

''We're not dealing with a logical, or rational, person. This guy is sick. He's also very intelligent, and patient enough to wait until circumstances meet his require-ments to enable him to get what he's after. Sophie, he's apparently decided, in his twisted mind, to play with you like a mouse caught in a trap—unsettle you, put you on edge, scare the hell out of you—before he makes his fi-nal move.''

''Don't try to protect me by softening the cold, hard facts, Tyson,'' Sophie said dryly. ''Just spit it out. Tell it like it is.''

''Oh,'' Tyson said, ''I'm sorry. I'm not well versed in beating around the bush, I guess. In my line of work, we have a tendency to get right to the point . . . one way or another.''

''Yes, but you don't work *all* the time. Do you have any family?''

''No.''

''I'm not just speaking of a wife, I mean parents, brothers, sisters.''

''No.''

''No one?''

''No, Sophie, no one.''

''I'm sorry,'' she said softly. ''That must be difficult, very lonely.''

"You really can't miss what you've never had." Tyson shrugged and changed the subject. "What are your plans for today?" he asked. "Are you scheduled to go out?"

Sophie looked directly at him for a long moment.

He hadn't moved, but yet, she realized, it was as though he'd stepped backward, and a wall had dropped between them. He obviously didn't like to talk about himself, reveal personal details of his life.

So, okay, she decided, she'd follow his rules for now. She'd learned social skills over the years like a good little girl, knew she should respect another person's right to privacy. But the woman in her, the purely feminine section of her being, wanted to know more, much more, about Tyson MacDonald.

Sophie, no, she admonished herself. She mustn't forget, not even for one single beat of her now-racing heart, that Tyson was one of them. He belonged to a world that she never intended to accept, ever again.

"Sophie, did you fall asleep on me?" Tyson said, snapping her back to attention. "What's your schedule for today?"

"What? Oh. I have to make a check on a project this afternoon. Some wallpaper was hung, and I don't pay for the labor until I have final inspection."

"What time?"

"Three o'clock."

"Don't leave here until I get back. I'll go with you to wherever this wallpaper is."

"Tyson, for heaven's sake, isn't that a bit dramatic? Are you saying you're about to become my bodyguard?"

"Close enough."

"That's ridiculous. How am I supposed to explain why you're with me?"

"We'll think of something. I'm a student who's getting on-the-job training."

Sophie's gaze flickered over Tyson's rugged features, then on to his wide shoulders, down to his muscled thighs outlined to perfection in faded jeans. And there, too, was that aura of blatant masculinity, that sensual something that was both exciting and frightening in the same breathless moment.

"You'd never pass as a student of interior design," she said, shaking her head. "There's just something about you that shouts the message that you need space, freedom, will do things the way *you* want to."

"I think I've been insulted. Well, don't worry about it. We'll come up with an idea between now and this afternoon. In the meantime, stay put."

"Where are you going?"

"To check out the florist shops around here. It's a long shot, but maybe someone will remember a customer who bought one flower and asked for an extra sheet of tissue. It's worth a try."

"Wouldn't it be easier to telephone?"

"I get better results in person."

"Yes," she said, smiling. "I imagine you do, Mr. MacDonald." Her smile faded. "You know, Tyson, I'm not certain that it's fully sunk in that there is someone out there who wants to..." She shivered. "Correct that. It *has* sunk in, and I'm scared to death. How's that for being brave, courageous and bold?"

"Hey," he said, then lifted one hand and drew his thumb over the soft skin of her cheek. "You're doing just fine, Sophie. Really great. Hank would be proud of you.

And remember that I'm here, okay? Nothing is going to happen to you. I'm going to make certain of that.''

Their eyes met, the stroking motion of Tyson's thumb stilled and there suddenly seemed to be nothing, no one, beyond the circle of space, the hazy, sensual cocoon that encased them. Eyes of summer-sky blue and those of rich dark brown, sent and received messages of heightened awareness and glowing, growing desire.

Then Tyson moved his hand from Sophie's cheek to the nape of her neck, stepped closer to her, lowered his head and kissed her.

And the kiss was ecstasy.

It was an instantaneous explosion of sensations, of heated desire that burst from an ember to a raging flame that consumed them. Tyson slipped his tongue between Sophie's lips to the sweet darkness within her mouth. She met his tongue eagerly as she returned the searing intensity of the kiss in total abandon.

Her knees began to tremble, and she gripped the lapels of Tyson's jacket for support. She couldn't think, could hardly breathe, was capable only of feeling, savoring. She tugged on Tyson's jacket, urging his mouth to press more forcefully onto hers, wanting more, giving more.

Voices bellowed in Tyson's mind, telling him to stop, warning him that he was slipping closer and closer to the edge of his control. Blood pounded in his veins. His manhood was heavy, aching with the want and need of Sophie. She smelled like sweet spice, tasted like honey and was pushing him over the brink of reason.

No!

Tyson tore his mouth from Sophie's and dropped his hand from her neck in the next instant. She pulled away slightly, then met his smoldering gaze. She blinked as though she were awakening from a dream-filled sleep.

"Well…" she said, realizing she had no more air in her lungs.

"Well…" Tyson said, a deep frown on his face.

He spun on his heel and strode across the room, leaving the house with the clatter of the bells echoing behind him.

Sophie stood statue-still, waiting for her heart to return to a normal cadence. She pressed her fingertips to her lips and closed her eyes.

No!

Her eyes flew open, and her hands became fists planted on her hips.

No, no, no, she told herself. She would *not* fall under the spell cast by Tyson MacDonald. She would *not* lose control of her emotions in regard to that man. To do so was guaranteed heartbreak.

She would *not* forget, not again, that Tyson was one of them.

Four

___

Sophie and Janet did not have an opportunity to speak again until the lull at noon when they both appeared in the kitchen.

"Goodness," Sophie said, opening the refrigerator door, "what a busy morning. Do you want to share the rest of this macaroni salad with me?"

"Sure," Janet said. "I'll do drinks. Tea? Coffee? Expensive imported champagne?"

"I think we're a tad short on champagne. Tea is fine. Let's brew up a pot of Earl Grey."

The pair was soon seated at the round wooden table at the far end of the kitchen, Janet having decided that toast fingers were needed to do the lunch justice.

"Okay," Janet said, "I've allowed you two bites of salad with no interrogation. That's all the time you're getting. Who is Tyson MacDonald?"

Sophie kept her eyes on the food in front of her. "He told you. I met him in the interior design class I'm teaching."

"When?"

"Last night. He just suddenly appeared in the classroom out of nowhere."

"Right. Certainly. That's why you knew he had the type of sense of humor to send the flower and the book. You peered into his brain while you were lecturing on passionate red."

"Well, he did come back to my apartment after class so we could—chat...get to know each other better. That's why I have an insight into his sense of humor."

"Now we're getting to the good part," Janet said, then took a bite of toast. "Tyson MacDonald is so scrumptious, I can hardly stand it. He sure doesn't seem like the type to be interested in interior decorating, though. What is he going to decorate?"

Sophie shrugged. "Beats me."

Janet narrowed her eyes. "Sophie Clarkson, you're keeping something from me, I can tell. What's going on between you and Tyson MacDonald?"

"Nothing," Sophie said quickly, still not looking at Janet. "Why would you assume there's something going on? Don't answer that. With your imagination you would naturally think there is a hot and heavy number in progress between me and Tyson."

"If there isn't, you're crazy." Janet laughed merrily. "Talk about a TDH."

"Janet, for heaven's sake," Sophie said, shooting her a quick glare, "I date several different men, and I'm seeing a lot of Todd, remember?"

"Ugh," she said, wrinkling her nose. "Todd is boring, stuffy, has memorized the manual on behaving in a manner befitting an upwardly mobile yuppie and never does one thing out of character."

"Todd is stable, is dedicated to the advancement of his career."

"Blah. Tyson MacDonald has great potential. I can't decide if he's a dark, brooding Heathcliff type, or a James Dean rebel type. Either way, he could eat crackers in my bed any time he felt the urge."

Sophie laughed. "You're terrible. Could we change the subject? How did it go with Mrs. Jameson?"

"I'd rather discuss Tyson MacDonald, but Mrs. Jameson picked what she wanted from the swatches, and I placed the order for the material. She's a joy to work with compared to some of our other OPAL."

"OPAL," Sophie said. "Give me a minute here. I know this one. OPAL. Oh, yes, Older Person with Active Lifestyle."

"Very good, Sophie," Janet said, beaming. "There's hope for you yet."

They finished lunch. Janet announced that she was off to take measurements of a room that was going to be turned into a nursery, but she'd be back to cover before Sophie was due to leave for the final inspection of the freshly hung wallpaper.

Oh, good grief, the wallpaper inspection, Sophie thought as Janet left the house. She still had no idea how she was going to explain why Tyson was with her. Well, she wouldn't dwell on that now, as it brought into sharp focus the fact that some lunatic was out there who was determined that she would die should she stand in his way to his obtaining the microdot. For all she knew, Jasco would kill her even if *he* had the microdot in his clutches.

Dear Lord, what a sick and twisted mind Jasco had, Sophie's thoughts rushed on. His anger directed toward

Hank Clarkson had festered and brewed for years, according to what Tyson had said. The burning hatred within Jasco had not been quelled with her father's death, because Jasco had yet to gain possession of the microdot. Now the focus was on *her* and the microdot.

She shivered as she wandered into the main area of Sophie's Attic and added another log to the fire. Her glance fell on the flower and book still sitting on the end table, and she tossed the flower into the fire, relieved to see the last of it turn into dark ashes.

She should burn the book, too, she decided, then hesitated. Tyson was attempting to discover where the flower had been purchased, with the hope that a clerk would remember the person who had bought it. Possibly, though it was a long shot at best, Jasco had said something that might give a clue as to where he was staying.

But what about the book? Sophie pondered. Shouldn't the same type of investigation be done regarding the book? She could hear the bells announcing that someone had come in. Yes, it was sound reasoning. She'd call the bookstores in the immediate area and ask if they stocked the little book and if they remembered anyone purchasing it.

With a decisive nod, she picked up the book and hurried into her office.

Tyson sat in the small café and stared into the dark, steaming liquid that had been advertised as coffee. His hands were wrapped around the heavy beige mug where it rested on the chipped Formica table.

He'd eaten a cheeseburger and fries, but had been so preoccupied, he hadn't really tasted it. Which was just as well, he decided, glancing around, considering the condition of the place and the odor of stale grease that hung in the air. But the waitress was friendly, the customers were laid-back and the time-worn café was, in actuality, his kind of place. He felt comfortable here and fit in.

And it was miles in distance, and a social level apart, from the world of Sophie Clarkson.

What difference did *that* make? he asked himself angrily a second later. Unless two people were contemplating a future together, their backgrounds, common interests, weren't important. He was *not* planning a future with Sophie, so he'd enjoy his coffee in the sleazy café where *he* belonged.

All that would add up to being exactly the way it was, pure and simple, if only he hadn't kissed her. Lord, that kiss. Incredible. It had been like . . . hell, he didn't know any fancy, romantic ways to describe a kiss that had turned him inside out.

Forget it, MacDonald, he told himself. Just forget it, and concentrate on the flower. The problem with that line of thinking was that he'd struck out at the seventeen flower shops he'd been to. None of them—not even one—had had any rhododendrons in stock in months. So he'd been unable to pursue the clue further, as to whether they remembered who'd bought one then asked for an extra sheet of tissue. Nice try, but no cigar.

Tyson glanced at his watch, then took one more swallow of coffee before getting to his feet. It was time to go back to Sophie's Attic and become a wallpaper inspector. It was time, he thought, to return to Sophie.

When Tyson entered the shop, Sophie appeared a second later. She stepped into the main area and stopped, a smile on her face.

Tyson's gaze flickered over the green, flared wool skirt she wore with a green-and-white-striped sweater and brown pumps. He had not, he now realized, paid any attention to what she was wearing when he'd been there earlier.

But he was definitely paying attention now, he thought dryly. Sophie looked sensational—a fact that he was determined to ignore.

"Ready to go?" Sophie said. "Janet just got back from an appointment. She's in the kitchen having a cup of tea to take off the chill." She crossed the room to stand in front of him and lowered her voice when she spoke again. "Janet is going to pop out here any second, and she'll want to know why you're going with me. Tyson, what should I say?"

"That we want to be together, I guess."

Sophie's eyes widened. "Are you kidding? Do you realize what that implies?"

He shrugged. "You were the one who said I'd never pull off the interior-decorating-student bit. So, we'll go with the wanting-to-be-together routine."

"Dandy," Sophie said, frowning. "If I can't stand being separated from you for the afternoon, how do we explain that I have a date with Todd Lexington tonight?"

"Cancel it."

"I certainly will not."

"Why not?" Tyson said, matching her frown. "Are you serious about this Todd guy? In love with him, daydreaming about mortgage, kids, a puppy and a station wagon?"

"Well, no, but... that's none of your concern, Mr. MacDonald."

"My concern," he said, a pulse beating wildly in his temple, "is to keep you safe. My concern is to make sure that the nut case who's wandering around out there doesn't kill you. My concern is—''

"All right," Sophie said, nearly yelling. She took a deep breath, let it out slowly and regained control of her temper. "I'll tell Todd that I have a client from out of town to entertain. But Janet knows differently and... Tyson, I'm a lousy liar. I'll trip myself up for sure."

"Well, Janet doesn't know I'm even here. I'll wait for you outside."

"Yes, okay. Did you have any luck at all at the flower shops?"

"No."

"I called twenty-two bookstores," she said, "but none carried *Dictionary of Flowers*."

"That was sharp thinking on your part, Sophie."

"It didn't help one bit."

"I'm still very impressed that you thought to do it. You're Hank's kid, all right. If you don't watch out, the State Department is liable to circle around and try to recruit you to fill your father's spot. Uh-oh, we blew it by standing here too long," Tyson smiled. "Hi, Janet, how's it going?"

"Hi, Tyson," she said. "I'm fine, now that my toes have defrosted. Sophie, you'll be late for sure if you don't get started. It's snowing harder, and the roads will most likely get sloppy. It's one of those wet snows, too, not a pretty stick-to-stuff snow."

"Yes, you're right," Sophie said. "I'll get my coat." She moved toward the stairs.

"Are you planning to stay and keep me company, Tyson?" Janet said.

"No. I thought I'd go along with Sophie and keep *her* company."

"Oh, how nice," Janet said, beaming. The front door opened and a man entered. "Oh, good grief."

Sophie came back down the stairs wearing her coat and carrying her purse. Her step faltered slightly when she saw who had come in during her brief absence. She managed a weak smile, then left the stairs.

"Todd," she said, "whatever are you doing here at this time of day?"

"I had to go right by, so I thought I'd drop in, have a cup of tea, make sure we're still on for tonight."

Todd Lexington was a clone of every yuppie attorney Tyson had ever seen. He was maybe five-ten, had drab-colored, light brown hair, drab-colored winter-white skin, wore a drab-colored gray suit and topcoat. The man was totally drab.

"Tea? Well, why don't you have a cup with Janet? I really must be on my way," Sophie said.

"I'm busy, busy, busy." Janet flapped her hands in the air. "No time for tea. Sorry, Todd. Bye, Todd. Sophie, you and Tyson run along."

Todd's head snapped around, and he looked at Tyson. Sophie chattered her way through introductions, but neither man offered to shake hands with the other.

"Todd," Sophie said, "it's about tonight. You see, I—"

"She can't keep her date with you," Tyson interrupted gruffly. "Sophie and I have business to discuss."

"Business?" Todd said, raising his eyebrows. "What kind of business?"

"It's none of *your* business what kind of business," Sophie said crossly. She shook her head. "I'm sorry, I didn't mean to snap at you, Todd. However, I do have to cancel our date for tonight."

"To conduct *business* with him?" Todd said, jerking his head in Tyson's direction.

"Yes, exactly," Sophie said. "In fact, we're off to look at wallpaper right now. Coming, Tyson?"

"Now, wait a minute," Todd said. "I have dinner reservations made and—I don't like this, Sophie."

"Todd, I sincerely apologize for breaking our date. I'm asking for your understanding regarding the fact that at times business must come first. You canceled a Sunday outing we once planned because an out-of-town client of yours arrived unexpectedly. I realize that you had no choice but—"

"That was different," Todd said.

Sophie frowned. "Why? My goodness, Todd, I've never known you to act this way. I'm seeing an unflattering side of you that I didn't realize existed. It's very disturbing to hear you imply that my career isn't nearly as important as yours."

"I'll imply anything I damn well please," Todd growled.

"That's enough, Lexington," Tyson said, his voice ominously low.

"Oh?" Todd said. "Well, maybe you and I should step outside, MacDonald."

Tyson stared up at the ceiling and shook his head. "I can't believe he actually said that."

"I'd like to speak with your privately, Sophie," Todd said, his face flushed with anger.

"No can do," Tyson said. "Sophie and I are late for a wallpaper date."

"Late for a wallpaper date," Janet said, wiggling her ample hips. "I like the beat. It'll make the top ten for sure."

"Sophie—" Todd said through clenched teeth.

"Let's hit the road, Sophie," Tyson said.

"She's not going anywhere with you, MacDonald," Todd said.

"Yes, Lexington, she is."

"Aaak!" Sophie screamed, shocking the group into silence.

"Lord," Todd said, covering his heart with one hand.

"You two," Sophie said, her eyes darting back and forth between Tyson and Todd, "are disgusting. You sound like little boys on the playground, squabbling over a toy. Well, I have a news flash. I'm not a toy. I'm a woman, and it will be a cold day in a very, very hot place before I go anywhere with either of you."

"Now, Sophie," Todd said, smiling, "calm down, darling, and—"

"Out!" she said, pointing to the door. "Now!"

"I'll call you later," Todd said, then hurried out the door.

Sophie turned to Tyson, narrowed her eyes, pursed her lips, then stomped out of the store.

"Whew," Tyson said. "She's a tad ticked off. Well, here I go, putting my life on the line."

"Good luck, Tyson," Janet said. "You are by far the better man. So win."

Tyson opened his mouth to protest Janet's choice of words, to tell her that she'd misinterpreted the confrontation between him and Todd Lexington. But in the next instant he realized that Sophie was on her way to her car and would soon be driving away without him. He ran out the door.

Sophie was muttering under her breath as she made her way cautiously across the sidewalk leading to the driveway. She fervently wished she'd had the good sense to put on her boots and grab her umbrella before storming out of the house with her grandly dramatic exit. The snow that was falling was more of an icy rain, forming puddles on the walk and soaking through her coat. She refused to think about what her hair must look like.

She was so furious at Tyson MacDonald and Todd Lexington that she could spit, she inwardly fumed. The nerve of those two haggling over her like a couple of mangy dogs determined to claim ownership of a bone.

Todd Lexington was a jerk, her mind rushed on. She'd fully expected him to flop down on the floor and kick his feet like a three-year-old having a tantrum.

Todd. She could have sworn he was taller, had wider shoulders, was better looking. But next to Tyson, Todd had paled, had seemed to shrink in size, as well as sophisticated demeanor.

The entire scene had been misconstrued by Todd and Janet, Sophie knew. It had appeared as though Tyson was staking a claim on his woman. Just as Todd had been. But that wasn't true. Tyson had simply been determined to secure his place by her side to properly perform his role of bodyguard.

And for some dumb reason, she admitted to herself, that was very depressing.

"Oh, blast," Sophie said as she stepped in a puddle.

"Sophie," Tyson called, "hold it."

"Shut up," she hollered, continuing on her way.

Tyson sprinted across the walk to her side, splashing cold water over her feet in the process.

"Go away," she said.

"Not a chance," he said. "I don't want you out alone. My car or yours?"

"I'm driving, Mr. MacDonald," Sophie said, glowering at him. "If you wish to accompany me, don't even think about speaking to me. Your behavior, as well as Todd's, was despicable and demeaning.''

"Yes, ma'am," he said, grinning at her. "Sorry, ma'am. Let's get out of this snow, or rain, or whatever the hell it is. I'll even open the car door for you... ma'am.''

Sophie ignored Tyson's words, wished to the heavens that her body wasn't so acutely aware of his presence, and went to the driver's side of her little red car. Tyson was right behind her. He reached around her and opened the door.

"Ma'am," he said, smiling and sweeping one arm in the air.

Sophie's anger diminished at the sight of Tyson's smile, and she shook her head as she laughed.

"You're a troublemaker, sir," she said as she slid behind the wheel.

"Me? Hey, it was drab Todd who was performing like a total jerk.''

He closed the door and ran around to the passenger side of the car. He opened the door and maneuvered himself onto the seat, pulling the door closed behind him.

"They make these things for midgets," he said. "Look, I'm sorry if I caused problems between you and Lexington.''

Sophie turned the key in the ignition. "It wasn't all your fault, Tyson." She backed out of the driveway and began to drive slowly along the slippery street. "I still find it hard to believe that Todd acted the way he did.''

Tyson shrugged. "From the beginning of time, men have been known to lose it over a woman. That's just the way it is.''

Sophie glanced quickly at Tyson, surprise at what he had said evident in her expression. She redirected her attention to the road.

Was Tyson including himself in that statement? Or were the walls he'd constructed around himself so high and strong that no woman would ever be able to break through to claim his heart?

The answer to the question was unimportant, she told herself. Tyson was a government agent, and she wanted no part of that world, ever again.

But still, she couldn't help but wonder what it would be like to love, be loved in kind, and make love with Tyson MacDonald.

Five

Two hours later, Sophie and Tyson drove away from the house where Sophie had conducted her inspection of the wallpaper. The fall of wet snow had stopped, leaving the quickly approaching night clear but bitterly cold. They had, at the invitation of Sophie's client, stood before a huge flagstone fireplace, the leaping flames warming the chill of their bodies and drying their clothes.

"Why don't you pick a place for us to get some dinner?" Tyson said. He glanced down at his jeans. "Make it casual. You're dressed to the nines, but I'm not."

"Yes, all right," Sophie said, keeping her eye on the surging traffic. "You know, it's amazing when I really think about how I continue to go through my normal work routine as though this nightmare of Jasco isn't actually happening. I guess we are usually more resilient than we give ourselves credit for."

"That's very true."

"Granted, at times the realization of the whole mess creeps up on me unexpectedly. I become terribly frightened again, scared to death. Then I do something like inspect wallpaper, and I feel myself relax a bit. Next I seem to shift, to take a step onto the road of 'mad as hell.' That's where I am right now, Tyson, angry, and very, very determined to find Jasco and bring him to justice."

"Fair enough," Tyson said, nodding. "Just don't let that anger make you reckless or cause you to act before you think. We're in this together, Sophie, and that means cooperating and communicating. Okay?"

"Yes."

We're in this together, Sophie, her mind echoed. Together . . . together . . . together. Sophie and Tyson together. Why did that sound so comforting, so special, so, so very right? Tyson didn't mean together in the sense of a romantic couple, man and woman. He was referring to being partners as he had been with Hank many times over the past years, nothing more.

She was, she admitted to herself, functioning as one of them, and intended to continue to do so until that lunatic was caught. She'd entered a world she'd stood in harsh judgment of and felt justified in being there.

"I see you're using Hank's key chain," Tyson said, pulling Sophie from her thoughts. "It's sure worse for wear. That's understandable, though, because it has covered a lot of miles with Hank."

And that key chain would go back into Hank's pocket where it belonged if he pulled through, he mused. He was still hanging in there, according to what Tyson had been told when he'd called in that morning.

Sophie was using the tattered memento as a loving tribute to her dead father. But Hank Clarkson was *alive*, and a painful fist twisted in Tyson's gut every time he thought about the lie he was living.

"Maybe I'll take the key chain to a jewelry store and see if they can polish the little ballerina charm." She paused. "No, on second thought, I think I'll leave it just as it was when it was my father's. Oh, that restaurant up ahead has delicious seafood. How does fish and chips sound to you?"

"Fine, fine," Tyson said absently, still looking at the key chain.

The restaurant was cozy and casual, as Tyson had requested. The theme was nautical, with fishnets hanging on the wall, and the waitresses in long gingham dresses and dust caps that depicted the era of the whaling boats and pubs. The tables, complete with captain's chairs, had brass hurricane lamps in the center, a candle glowing in each.

They were shown to a table, ordered, and were soon eating their first course of a crisp, tasty salad.

"We can talk about the situation," Tyson said between bites, "or put it on hold for now—whatever feels right to you."

"I have a few questions, then I'd like to just enjoy the meal."

"Okay."

"Tyson, how would Jasco know about me and where I live?"

"It wouldn't be difficult. We don't carry anything with personal identification while we're on an assignment, but the underground network of the less than wonderful types has as much information on us as we do on them. We'd be kidding ourselves if we thought differently."

"I see," she said slowly. "Then it stands to reason that Jasco has recognized you as you've come and gone from my house and Sophie's Attic."

Tyson nodded. "Guaranteed. The creep probably knows exactly where the outside agent I've assigned to watch your place is stationed, too."

"So, in essence, you and Jasco are taunting each other. You're saying, 'Here I am,' and he's toying with you *and* me by managing to put that flower by my door. It's an interesting, though dangerous, duel of sorts."

Tyson looked at Sophie for a long moment before he spoke.

"You think so much like Hank that it's uncanny. You're very detail oriented."

"Those traits have made me a good businesswoman. However, I have to admit that for all my condemnation of your work, I'm right smack-dab in the middle of it myself. The thought of being left on the sidelines and simply reported to is unacceptable. I guess you're right, Tyson, I'm a hypocrite."

The waitress reappeared at their table and set seafood platters in front of them. Coffee was poured, Tyson said everything was fine and the woman smiled and moved away. Sophie and Tyson ate in silence for several minutes.

"This is great," Tyson finally said.

"Yes, it is, and I'm realizing how hungry I was. Tyson, let's put Jasco on a back burner for now. My dad never told me specifics about his work on the criminals he dealt with. I realize that the majority were evil, but weren't there some who were colorful, unusual, the kind they show in the movies? Just for fun, tell me about a few of those?"

"Fun?" Tyson chuckled and shook his head. "I swear, Sophie, when you switch boats in the middle of the stream, you pack all your luggage and go for it."

"That's the only way I know how to do things, Tyson. It's one hundred percent, or just forget it. I'm Hank's kid."

"You are, indeed."

"I'll be shifting back to my original boat when this is over, of course, hypocrite that I am."

"Are you certain about that?" Tyson asked quietly, looking directly into her eyes.

Oh, drat, Sophie thought, her heart beating like a wild bongo drum. When Tyson pinned her in place with those brown eyes of his, she was thrown for a loop.

"Well, yes, of course I'm certain," she said, hearing the thread of breathlessness in her voice. "I mean, heavenly days, I'm not about to sign up to be an agent."

"No?"

"Tyson, just stick to the subject. Didn't you ever deal with some crooks who would be great with James Bond?"

Tyson laughed. "Okay, let's see here. Hank and I broke up a diamond-smuggling ring years ago. The kingpin was named Walter Jensen. He's short, maybe five-six, and round as a cue ball. The truth is, the creep has a cherub face, could pass for Santa Claus. His trademark was a white suit with a pink carnation in the lapel. He always wore that."

Sophie leaned slightly toward him. "Really? He looks like Santa Claus?"

"Yep."

"I love it. Okay, who's next?"

"There was a woman named Zula. No last name. She was the woman, wife, I don't know, of a master counterfeiter who had an operation so big it boggled the mind. We blew it apart. Zula was part Spanish, I think, had dark hair, olive-toned skin. She'd be about forty now. Back then she was beautiful, really stunning. She wore sparkling caftans, or whatever you call those things, and a lot of bright bracelets, rings, earrings. The guys used to say she was the best-looking crook we ever hauled in. Actually she never went to jail because there wasn't enough evidence against her. She was guilty as the day was long, but I don't know what happened to her. And that, Ms. Clarkson, is enough of a cast for James Bond.''

"Well, darn,'' Sophie said, smiling. Her smile slowly faded. "What does Jasco look like?''

Tyson sighed. "Back to business, huh? Jasco is sleazy, thin, nervous and very hyper. He has a small frame and a weird, sort of eerie-sounding laugh. He'd be in his late forties now, I guess.''

"What happened between him and my father years ago that made Jasco so angry?''

"Jasco was to assassinate an important diplomat from a country I'll leave unnamed. It was to appear to have been the work of a group from another country, and would have blown some very delicate negotiations. Anyway, Hank and I had tips as to where Jasco was. I checked out one place, Hank the other. Hank found him.''

"What happened?''

"Sophie, look, you don't need a blow-by-blow accounting of—''

"Tyson,'' she interrupted, "tell me.''

He hesitated, then finally spoke. "Yeah, okay. Short and not so sweet. Jasco had his ever-famous knife. He came after Hank, they fought. Hank got the knife and ended up cutting the right side of Jasco's face from his eye all the way down to along his mouth. Jasco has an ugly, puckered, discolored scar.''

''Oh,'' Sophie whispered.

Tyson leaned forward, then reached across the table and covered one of her hands with one of his.

''Damn,'' he said, ''I shouldn't have told you about that.''

''Yes, I wanted to know. Thank you, Tyson.''

He looked directly into her eyes as he began to stroke the side of her hand with his thumb in a slow, steady rhythm.

Dear heaven, Sophie thought, the heat from Tyson's strong but gentle hand was traveling up her arm and across her breasts, causing them to tingle, feel heavy, yearning for his soothing touch. And the rhythm of his thumb matched a pulsing tempo deep within her.

She wanted Tyson to kiss her, capture her mouth with his, repeat the ecstasy of before. She wanted to press her soft body to the hard contours of his, inhale his aroma, savor his taste. She wanted to make love with this man through the long, secret hours of the night.

''Tyson . . .'' she said, not even realizing she'd spoken aloud.

He frowned, then straightened, jerking his hand from hers.

How long had she held him mesmerized? he wondered. Great agent he was. The room had faded into oblivion as he saw only Sophie. A whole band of terrorists could have marched through the restaurant and he'd never have known it.

How he desired her.

He was on fire, burning, aching with need, aching with wanting Sophie. Each time she cast her spell over him, he had a more difficult time regaining control, inching back to reality and reason. Nothing like this had ever happened to him before.

"I…" Tyson started, then cleared his throat. "Do you want dessert?"

Sophie shook her head slightly to clear the sensuous mist that seemed to be hovering over her. The room returned to view, and the chatter of voices and clatter of dishes reached her.

"Dessert?" she repeated. "Oh, no, thank you. I couldn't eat another thing."

"We might as well get going, then. Just one thing, Sophie."

"Yes?"

"Todd Lexington. He's jealous as hell—you realize that."

"Yes," she said, wearily, "but he's assuming too much regarding what he thinks we have together. We haven't made any kind of commitment, haven't come even remotely close to discussing a future."

"Well, what I'm trying to find out here is if you plan to attempt to patch things up with him. You know, soothe his ruffled feathers."

Sophie frowned. "Todd's attitude and actions when he met you are very distressing to me, but I can't deal with it all right now. I've enjoyed his company, and we had some very pleasant outings. I guess I was grieving so much for my father, I missed the signals that Todd was moving forward much faster than I was. But to really answer your question, Tyson, no, I'm not going to approach Todd now. I intend to concentrate on doing my part to apprehend Jasco."

"That's good," Tyson said, signaling to the waitress for the check.

"Why?"

He met her gaze directly. "Because we're going to stop at my hotel so I can check out. Then, Ms. Clarkson, as of tonight, I'm going to be living with you."

Six

Sophie Clarkson, Tyson thought, was making him very, *very* nervous.

He slid yet another glance in her direction, once again seeing the shuttered expression on her face as she drove. There was no visible clue as to what she was thinking, and it was extremely disconcerting.

Even worse, he mused on, she had not said one word, *not one,* since he'd announced his intention to move in with her. She'd simply stared at him for a long moment, settled a semibored look over her features, and that had been that.

He had not attempted to engage her in conversation as they left the restaurant. He'd announced the name of his hotel, and off they'd gone, with Sophie behind the wheel of her made-for-midgets car.

She had sat in a chair in his hotel room, idly flipping through a magazine while he'd packed. She'd given the appearance of someone who was completely relaxed, didn't have a care in the world, and who was just passing time by scanning a hotel-provided publication on the tourist attractions of Chicago.

It was like being in the close proximity of a time bomb, Tyson mentally continued, not knowing when it was going to explode nor having any idea as to what the outcome would be when it did.

Oh, yes, Sophie Clarkson was making him very, *very* nervous.

Sophie pulled into her driveway, turned off the ignition and left the car. Tyson retrieved his suitcase and strode after her. As she arrived at the top of the stairs and reached forward to insert the key in the lock on the door, he finally spoke.

"Hold it," he said. "I want to go in first and check things out."

Sophie handed him the key. Tyson entered the house, set his suitcase on the floor, then turned on the lights. Sophie stepped just inside the door, closed it behind her, then clasped her hands loosely as she gazed off into space. Tyson finally returned to stand about four feet in front of her.

"All clear," he said.

Sophie moved around him, tended to her coat and purse, slipped off her shoes, then sat down in the fan-backed chair. Tyson frowned, shrugged out of his jacket and dropped it onto the end of the sofa. He sat down on the other end, then got to his feet again in the next instant.

"Would you like me to start a fire?" he asked.

"That would be lovely," she said, intently studying the condition of her fingernails.

Tyson set about his task, grateful for something to do while waiting for the time bomb to detonate. Sophie's disturbing and confusing behavior had taken a toll from him, he soon realized. He juggled a log that ended up landing on his foot, went through half a book of matches before he could get one to light, then nearly forgot to set the screen back in place in front of the now-crackling flames.

He finally straightened, folded his arms tightly across his chest and glowered at Sophie.

"Damn it, Sophie," he said, "would you knock it off?"

She looked up at him, an expression of pure innocence on her face. "I beg your pardon?"

"You're driving me crazy," he said, his voice rising. "I'd rather face three thugs in an alley than this, this whatever it is that you're doing. At least there'd be no doubt as to what was on the hoods' minds. Yell, throw something at me, tell me to take a flying leap, or to go to hell, or... I've really had enough of this. I'm warning you, Sophie Clarkson, you've pushed me to the wall."

Sophie laughed. She laughed until she had to wrap her arms around her stomach. She laughed until she had tears in her eyes and was gasping for breath.

Each time she struggled for control, she'd look at the expression of building fury on Tyson's face, and off she'd go again, peals of laughter dancing through the air and filling the room to overflowing.

"Oh, dear me." She drew a deep breath. "Oh, my."

"Are you finished?" Tyson asked stiffly.

"Goodness, I hope so," she said, a wide smile on her face. "My stomach hurts."

Tyson slouched onto the sofa, his frown still firmly in place. "Would you care to explain your performance?"

"Hoist with one's own petard," Sophie said merrily. "I gotcha, MacDonald."

"What are you talking about?"

"My father once told me," she said, her smile beginning to fade, "that during training you're told that many times it proves beneficial to do the exact opposite of what is probably expected. You were ready to go ten rounds with me when I pitched my fit about your moving in here. So—" she shrugged "—I didn't pitch it. And you, sir, are a nervous wreck. You have just witnessed the teachings of Hank Clarkson being put into action."

A slow smile crept onto Tyson's face and grew into a grin. He chuckled and shook his head.

"Sophie," he said, "you're right, you got me good. Hank did a fine job of raising you."

"He was a wonderful father," she said quietly.

"Yeah," Tyson said, no longer smiling. "You . . . lost him sooner than you should have, but the years you had together were special. You have terrific memories of your time with him, and those memories are important."

"I know. Oh, believe me, I know that, Tyson. Every one of those moments is tucked away in Sophie's attic."

"What?"

"Ever since I was a little girl, my dad would tell me the same story. Oh, how I loved to hear it, would beg him to tell me again and again. It was something my mother told him, saying it was passed on from *her* mother, and her mother before that."

"Go on."

"'Soapy,' Hank would say, 'there's a secret cupboard in your heart that belongs to just you. Your mother taught me about it, and now I have one, too. Mine is Hank's attic, yours is Sophie's attic, your mother's was Hannah's attic, and on the list goes. It's there, in that special, private space, the attic of your heart, that you tuck away thoughts and memories to cherish. When I want to think about your mother, I reach into my attic and, sure enough, there are the beautiful memories of my beloved Hannah.'"

A gentle smile touched Sophie's lips.

"'And when I'm away from you,' he'd continue, 'I know my attic is bursting at the seams with thoughts and memories of you, Soapy.'" Her smile misted with tears. "And then he'd say that there was room in the attic of everyone's heart for hopes, and dreams, and wishes made on birthday candles, and the first star light, star bright, first star that twinkles in the sky if someone stops long enough to wait and watch for it to appear."

A single tear slid down one cheek, and she brushed it away.

"Oh, how I loved that story. As I grew older, I *did* have a dream. I wanted, I was determined to have, my own interior-decorating business. I worked very hard toward that goal, and when I achieved it, it was as natural as breathing to name it Sophie's Attic."

She turned her head to stare into the flames of the fire, lost in her own thoughts of days past.

Tyson stared at her, seeing the fire's glow change her hair to the color of gleaming copper, seeing her dewy skin become the shade of a sun-kissed peach. An achy sensation in his throat and chest told him that tears he wouldn't shed were making their presence known.

And he was shaken to the very core of his being.

What Sophie had just shared with him, the words she'd spoken in a voice filled with love for Hank, had touched him in a place within that he hadn't known he possessed. A warmth like nothing he'd ever experienced before spread through him.

And in that moment, while sitting in Sophie's living room, Tyson knew that his life had been irrevocably changed. He was consumed by the greatest joy, and the greatest fear, he had ever known.

"Well," Sophie said, bringing herself back from the memory-filled place her mind had taken her to.

Tyson blinked with the hope of clearing his jumbled mind, but his heart continued to beat with a wild cadence, and a trickle of sweat ran down his back.

"Tyson?" Sophie said.

"What? Oh, I . . . that was a nice story you told me," he said, hearing the gritty quality of his voice. "Really nice. Thank you, Sophie, for sharing it with me."

Their eyes met, and desire flared as brightly and as heated as the flames in the hearth. Neither spoke, nor moved.

Tyson, Sophie's heart and mind whispered. He was weaving his magic spell again, pulling her to him by invisible, sensual threads. Her breasts were heavy, achy, and desire thrummed throughout her, swirling, pulsing low within her.

She wanted to make love with this man, to have the power of that magnificent body consume her, lift her up and away from reality. Oh, yes, she wanted Tyson, but even more, she *needed* him to fill a void in her life that she hadn't known existed.

Oh, Sophie, stop and think, she admonished herself. If she succumbed to her yearnings, she was going to pay a piper who would demand a tremendous price. Facts were facts: Tyson was an agent, and she couldn't live in that world, not ever again. Tyson was the wrong man for her.

Sophie tore her gaze from Tyson's.

"So!" she said, forcing a lightness into her voice that she didn't feel. "Are you ready to slug it out, Mr. MacDonald?"

Tyson blinked again, dispelling the sensual haze that had surrounded him.

"What?" he said, frowning slightly.

Sophie drummed her fingertips on the arms of the chair. "My dear man, you don't actually believe that I'm going to submissively sit here and allow you to take up residence in my home, do you?"

The time bomb, Tyson thought dryly, was about to explode.

"Yeah," he said, slowly nodding, "that's how it's going to be. It's not even up for a vote."

"Is that a fact?" Sophie said, folding her arms beneath her breasts. "Well, think again, Tyson MacDonald. Don't overtax your brain in the process, but you might give a thought to the status of my reputation."

Tyson shrugged. "We've already covered that detail. You said yourself that you have no commitment to Todd Lexington. I'm glad you're beginning to realize that he isn't that great a catch. I mean, we're talking about one very drab guy there. Very drab."

"Damn you, Tyson, this has ramifications far beyond Todd Lexington."

"You shouldn't swear like that, Sophie. Hank wouldn't approve."

"Just what do you suggest I tell Janet? She's my best friend, remember? She knows it would be completely out of character for me to start living with a man I've only known for a handful of days."

"Love, say the experts, is a powerful thing. You tell Janet that...wham...we fell in love, went down for the count. Yeah, there we go, nice and neat. We're in love with each other.''

Which wasn't true, of course, Tyson told himself. No way. Granted, *something* was happening between him and Sophie, but it sure as hell wasn't love.

"Look," Tyson said, "I know my moving in here isn't the best solution for you because you have friends who are going to ask questions, but this plan is the best I have to offer. Jasco isn't about to change his mind and ride off into the sunset. He's very clever and very patient. We can't let down our guard for one minute. I'm sorry if your reputation gets blown to smithereens, but better it than you. Besides, in this day and age, I can't picture people passing harsh judgment on our living arrangements.''

Sophie sighed, a very weary-sounding sigh.

"No, I don't suppose they'll point fingers once they get over their initial surprise. I just hate to lie, especially to Janet." She threw up her hands. "But I have to face the fact that I need a bodyguard. Lord, what a nightmare.'' She shivered.

"We'll get Jasco, Sophie," Tyson said quietly. "I promise you that.''

"*We'll* get him?''

"If that's the way you still want it. I respect your right to be as involved as you wish in this. Hank is…was your father, and now *your* life is in danger. I'm assuming you'd follow my orders to the letter if things get tense. By the same token, if you'd rather pull back, keep a low profile, let me do this on my own, I'll respect that, too. There'd be no shame in that—you don't have to prove anything to anyone. You haven't even been trained in this type of work, but… No, forget it.''

"But what? Finish the sentence.''

"I don't know, you just have the knack, the instinct. You've inherited Hank's sixth sense, or whatever. I've *never* involved a civilian in anything like this. Maybe I'm way off base to do it now, but ... well, I just think we'd make a good team."

Sophie smiled. "Like Bonnie and Clyde?"

"No way," Tyson said, matching her smile. "We're the guys in the white hats." He paused, and his smile faded. "What's on for tomorrow? Is Sophie's Attic open on Saturday?"

"By appointment only. There are some people who find it impossible to get here during the work week. There are no appointments on the calendar for tomorrow, but I'm going to an auction up north. Oh, I just realized that I won't see Janet over the weekend. We'll simply have to catch Jasco before Monday morning so I don't have to lie to her about why you're living here."

"Oh, okay," Tyson said, chuckling. "We'll nab him in the next forty-eight hours. Now, let's back up to the auction and give me some details."

"There's a barn that a couple bought several years ago and established as the permanent place to hold their auctions. The husband and wife travel across the country collecting things until they have enough to hold an auction. They send out notices to interior decorators, private people who have asked to be on their list and so on. I'm doing a country kitchen for a woman and hope to find some authentic pieces to go with the decor."

"I see," Tyson said. "What time do we leave here?"

"You're going with me? Well, yes, I guess you are. I'd like to be on the way by eight tomorrow morning. It's about a two-hour drive. The auction starts at eleven, so that gives me a chance to do a preview inspection of what is going to be sold. I hope the weather doesn't go bad, making it difficult to drive. We'll have some back-country roads to travel on.''

"I'll drive the car I've rented."

"No, I—"

"Sophie, please," Tyson said with a moan, "give me a break. That's a long haul when I'm sitting there with my knees in my mouth."

"Good point. You'll drive." She got to her feet. "I realize it's rather early, but I'm exhausted. There's a second bedroom up here that I've made into a den and guest room. I'll get you some bed linens and towels. The love seat in there pulls out into a single bed. You can use the bathroom in the hallway."

"Okay."

Tyson rose and crossed the room to pick up his suitcase. He followed Sophie down a short corridor. As she entered a small room, she flicked on a light.

Tyson glanced around, nodding in approval, not having taken the time to really appreciate the room when he checked things out when they'd first arrived. The color scheme, he realized, was totally different from the rest of the house and created a unique, warm atmosphere.

Dark wood bookshelves lined two walls, and there didn't appear to be space for one more book. The love seat was upholstered in a nubby, oatmeal-colored material, and a big, wrap-itself-around-you-appearing chair was burnt orange with a matching ottoman. A dark wood end table and lamp were next to the chair, a matching set by the love seat.

"I like this," Tyson said.

"So did my father," Sophie said. "He always complained that the living room was too feminine. Whenever he came over, we ended up settling in and chatting in here. I'll get the linens."

Sophie left the room, and Tyson set his suitcase on the floor. He moved forward, his attention caught by a framed photograph on the end table next to the chair. It was a picture of Sophie and Hank that was slightly off center and a bit blurry, but showed them standing in front of a Christmas tree. Hank's arm was across Sophie's shoulders, hers around his waist, and they were smiling.

"That was taken last Christmas," Sophie said as she reentered the room. "Janet took it. She's not the best photographer in the world, but I really like it."

"I can see why," Tyson said, turning to look at her. "You're both obviously very happy."

"My dad adored Christmas. He was terrible about sneaking peeks at presents, couldn't be trusted one iota. One year I locked his gifts in the trunk of my car until the very last minute, and he said that was cheating. I have some wonderful memories of our Christmases together over the years."

"And those memories are in Sophie's attic in your heart," Tyson said quietly.

"Yes. Yes, that's exactly where they are." She hesitated a moment. "And you? Do you have a Tyson's attic?"

"No."

"It's never too late to discover it's there."

"I just wouldn't have anything to put in it, Sophie."

"Yes, you would. You simply don't know how yet."

"Maybe."

They continued to look directly into each other's eyes, a half a room apart. Yet the distance between them seemed somehow to disappear even though neither moved. Sensuality heightened, was a nearly palpable entity. Hearts began to race, heat within them began to churn, and desire began to consume them.

Sophie's hold tightened on the linens she held in her arms as if the sheets and towels could act as a protective barrier between her and Tyson.

"I'll make up the bed," she finally said, her voice a near whisper.

"I'll, um, I'll help you."

Sophie nodded, and they performed the simple task of making up the single bed, each concentrating on the crisp sheets and fluffy blanket. They kept their eyes averted; neither one spoke.

And the air seemed to crackle like a high intensity electrical wire, from the ever-growing awareness and desire weaving around them.

Sophie put the pillow in place, smoothed the pillowcase, fiddled with the edge of the blanket, then slowly straightened and met Tyson's gaze where he stood looking at her from the opposite side of the bed.

They moved at the same time, as though pulled by invisible strings, and met at the end of the bed. Still without speaking, Sophie stepped into Tyson's embrace, and his arms encircled her, nestling her close to his body. Her arms lifted of their own volition to his neck, her fingertips inching into the thick depths of his dark hair. His mouth melted over hers in a searing kiss.

Emotions foreign and new began to take form within Tyson.

Protectiveness... Yes, he mused. He would protect Sophie against harm, stand between her and anything or anyone who might intend to hurt her.

Possessiveness... Yes. Sophie was his now, placed in his care by what had happened to Hank. Sophie was his, but not like a daughter to a father. No, she was a woman, and he, Tyson MacDonald, was a man.

Desire ... Yes. The heat churning low in Tyson's body increased as he became aware of Sophie's lush breasts, which were crushed to the hard wall of his chest. This longing within him now was deeper, richer, held far more meaning than simple lust. This wasn't crude carnal want; it was the aching need to mesh his body with Sophie's and be assured of her pleasure before he sought his own release.

And with all the new emotions came ...

Fear ... He was strong, tough and smart. He had stayed alive when the odds said he should be dead, had fine-tuned his body, mind, instincts, to razor sharpness. He was a formidable foe in the dark side of life, where no rules counted and death greeted those who dared to relax even for a moment.

But Tyson knew, as the cold sweat of fear dotted his forehead, that he could be cut off at the knees—rendered vulnerable, bare, with no shield to protect him—if he fell under the spell of this delicate creature in his arms, if he succumbed to the lure of Sophie.

And he could not, would not, allow that to happen.

The tip of Sophie's tongue met his, and a sensuous purr hummed in her throat as she leaned even more against Tyson's aroused body.

All rational thought fled Tyson's mind. He broke the kiss only long enough to draw a rough breath, then captured her mouth again, his tongue delving deep within.

Tyson, Sophie's mind and heart echoed over and over. *Tyson.*

She filled her senses with his taste and aroma and the feel of his hard muscled body. Their tongues dueled and danced, stroked in a sensuous tempo that ignited the fire deep within her even more. She was consumed with desire, and a need beyond description in its intensity.

"I want you, Tyson," she said, close to his lips.

"Oh, Sophie, yes."

An urgency engulfed them, a need so great it defied reason. Clothes were an encumbrance, a barrier that could not be tolerated. They shed their garments, allowing them to fall where they may, then stood naked before each other, offering all that they were.

Sophie's heart raced as she looked at Tyson, etching every detail of his magnificent body indelibly in her mind. His shoulders were so wide, his arms perfectly proportioned to his chest, which was covered in moist, dark curls. His powerful legs had corded muscles that gave evidence to his strength, and his manhood was fully aroused.

"Oh, Tyson," she whispered, "you're so beautiful."

"You, Sophie," he said, his voice raspy, "you're the beautiful one. You, you're the loveliest woman I've ever seen."

He stepped close again, cupping her lush breasts in his hands, savoring the soft bounty. His thumbs stroked the nipples gently, bringing them to taut buttons.

A soft sigh of pure, feminine pleasure escaped from Sophie's lips.

Tyson lifted her into his arms, laid her on the narrow bed, then stretched out next to her. He rested on one forearm, his gaze sweeping over her feminine beauty once more before splaying one hand on her flat stomach.

He kissed her deeply, his tongue plummeting to meet hers. Then he raised his head to seek one breast, drawing the sweet flesh into his mouth, flicking his tongue over the nipple.

Sophie wove her fingers into the damp thickness of his hair, urging his mouth more firmly onto her breast. The steady rhythm of his tongue was matched by the pulsing heat low, so low, within her.

He moved to her other breast, and she closed her eyes to fully savor the sensations swirling within her. Tyson's hand skimmed over her as his mouth continued its tantalizing, maddening foray. His fingers slid down the side of her leg, then up to the essence of her womanhood, touching, claiming as his, stroking until she was burning with desire.

He captured her mouth again in a searing kiss that seemed to steal the very breath from her body. Her hand slid over his glistening back, feeling the muscles bunch beneath her palm, trembling as he strove to hold himself in check. He lifted his head to meet her gaze.

"Please, Tyson," she said, her voice unsteady. "I want you so very, very much."

He gazed at her for another long moment, as though unable to get his fill of the beauty of her.

Then he moved over her and into her, consuming her, bringing to her welcoming dark haven all that he was as man. Deeper, deeper, and she received him, all of him, as woman.

And then he began to move, slowly at first, then increasing the tempo. She matched his cadence, wrapping her legs around his thighs, lifting her hips, wanting... wanting...

On and on they thundered, the pressure building, coiling tighter, as bodies glistened and hearts beat wildly. Higher they soared, reaching for the final ecstasy beyond the wondrous sensations that now engulfed them.

Higher, then higher yet, then...

They were flung into oblivion seconds apart, clinging to each other as the glorious spasms swept through them. They called to each other, saying the name of the only one who mattered, the only one who could travel to where they had gone then safely return.

"Tyson," Sophie said, tightly clutching his shoulders. "Oh, Tyson."

"Sophie, my Sophie."

They hovered there, suspended in time and space, then slowly drifted back. Tyson collapsed against her, sated, spent, his life's force having passed from him to her. She circled his back with her arms, holding fast as the last rippling spasms within her quieted.

Slowly, so slowly, the cloud of passion faded, revealing stark reality to Tyson. He started to move away, only to feel Sophie's arms tighten around him. He lifted his head to meet her gaze, his breath catching as he saw the lovely flush on her cheeks and the gentle smile on her lips.

"So wonderful," she said. "So very, very special."

"Yes. Yes, it was, but..."

"Shh. Please, Tyson, don't. This is our night to cherish. My memories of what we shared will be placed carefully in my Sophie's attic in my heart. Please don't spoil it by saying it shouldn't have happened, or by bringing the outside world into this exquisite place we created together."

Tyson looked at her for another long moment before he spoke. "All right, I won't say anything." He paused. "I've got to get off of you, Sophie, before I crush you."

She released her hold on him, and he settled next to her.

"Tyson," Sophie said, "this bed is too narrow for two people to sleep comfortably. Come to my room."

"No. You go on, sleep in your own bed, but I'll stay here."

"Why?"

"It's better this way, Sophie. If I'm in the same bed with you, I'll want you again and again through the night. You won't get any sleep."

"How delicious," she said, smiling. Her smile faded as she saw his frown deepen. "Oh, Tyson, you *are* regretting that this happened, aren't you? That's why you want me to go."

"I agreed not to talk about it. Sophie, look, my mind is a mess right now. It really would be best if you went to your own room. But believe this...I won't forget this night, not ever."

Sophie kissed him quickly on the lips. She slipped from the bed, gathered her clothes into a bundle in her arms, then turned with a smile to look at him. "Good night, Tyson."

"Sleep well, Sophie," he said, then watched her as she left the room.

Tyson turned out the light, then sank back onto the pillow. He laced his hands beneath his head and stared up at a ceiling he couldn't see in the darkness.

He'd meant what he'd said to Sophie, he thought. He wouldn't forget this night. Their lovemaking had been like nothing he'd experienced before. Wonderful? The word wasn't big enough, rich or full enough. It was, at least in *his* limited romantic vocabulary, beyond description.

But he also knew that what had taken place had thrust him into a dangerous arena where he didn't belong. For the first time in his life, emotions had played a very vital part of the sex act, changing it into making love, a joining that had been special, rare, and should be cherished.

Oh, yeah, he thought dryly, his mind was definitely a mess.

There were only two facts that were there in crystal clarity, and both caused a knot to tighten in his gut. He had to return to safe emotional ground where he was in command, had total control of himself, and he must *not* make love with Sophie Clarkson again.

Seven

Sophie awoke to the sound of water running in the shower in the bathroom off the hallway. As she blinked away the last traces of the fogginess of sleep, she smiled, vividly recalling every detail of the wondrous lovemaking shared with Tyson.

Her smile faded as she frowned slightly, deep in thought. When she'd slipped under the blankets the previous night, she'd fallen asleep within moments after her head had touched the pillow. She'd been sated, content and aglow with happiness.

But in the light of the new day, she decided, she was due for a mental inventory. Some women would, no doubt, be crushed to the core by Tyson's after-the-fact attitude, his "go to your room" dictate.

Sophie stretched leisurely, her eyes widening as she felt the soreness in places that were further evidence of the exquisite joining between her and Tyson. She pulled the blankets up to her chin and forced her mind back to serious thinking.

She was not, she knew, the least bit upset by Tyson's dismissal of her the previous night. No, far from it. What on the surface might appear to be abrupt and rather cold, she viewed in an entirely different light.

She was convinced Tyson had been deeply moved on an emotional plane by what had transpired. He was shaken, vulnerable. He had been unable to scramble behind his high, strong barrier before she'd witnessed his confusion and near fear over what he was feeling.

Oh, no, she wasn't crushed. She was ecstatic. She had managed to chip away some of Tyson's protective wall.

Sophie frowned again.

Whoa, madam, she admonished herself. She was definitely getting carried away. There was nothing to celebrate because the overall picture remained the same. She and Tyson had no possibility of a future together. None.

That he was an agent was a fact that hadn't changed. That he would leave once Jasco was apprehended was a given. That she was going to cry when he walked out of the door for the last time was etched in stone.

Well, dandy, she thought, much more of this type of thinking would cause her to be totally depressed. She had to decide—now—exactly what she intended to do while Tyson was still there.

Since her tears were going to flow unchecked, she reasoned, she might as well go for the gusto, gather as many beautiful memories as she could to tuck into Sophie's attic.

She would cherish every moment left to them, rejoicing in the sight of Tyson, the rich timbre of his laughter, the aroma that was his alone, the feel of his strong arms holding her fast. She would make love with him over and over. Beautiful, wonderful love that she could relive in her mind in the dark, lonely nights after Tyson was gone.

"So be it," she said aloud.

The sound of running water stopped, and Sophie went into the bathroom. She was soon standing under the stinging spray of the shower in her own bathroom. She washed quickly, then dried with a big, fluffy towel. She dressed, made the bed, applied light makeup, brushed her hair and left the bedroom in search of Tyson.

The aroma of freshly brewed coffee greeted her, and she headed for the kitchen. At the kitchen door she stopped, her heart skipping a beat, a shiver coursing through her as she looked at Tyson. He was standing with his back to her, his legs slightly spread in a blatantly masculine pose as he stared out the window.

Her gaze flickered over him, missing nothing, etching each detail indelibly in her mind. Oh, yes, she thought dreamily, there was Tyson. There were those wide shoulders in a steel gray sweater. Those long muscular legs encased in jeans, curving so enticingly over that nice, *nice* tush.

"Good morning," she said, refusing to believe that her voice had actually squeaked.

Tyson turned to face her. "Good morning. It snowed during the night. There seems to be quite a bit on the ground out there."

Oh, damn, he thought, look at her. Look at beautiful, sensational Sophie. She was wearing a silky, long-sleeved green blouse tucked into tight jeans that were encircled at her small waist by a brown leather belt.

And those long, lush legs of hers. Man, oh, man, those legs in jeans were sinful. To add to his agony, she was wearing butter-soft, brown leather boots that came to midcalf with the jeans inside. Hell, she was gorgeous. He was a dying man.

"Coffee?" he asked gruffly. "It's ready."

"Do you eat breakfast?" Sophie said.

He shrugged. "I can take it or leave it."

"There's bread if you want toast," she said. "I don't keep breakfast supplies on hand, because I just have coffee and popcorn."

"Popcorn?"

"Yes, popcorn."

She took a plastic container and a bowl from the cupboard and shook a hefty serving of popcorn into the bowl. She added milk and sugar, poured a cup of coffee and headed for the table, carrying her meal.

"Help yourself," she said, "to whatever strikes your fancy."

"Sophie, I have to ask. Why are you eating popcorn for breakfast?"

"It's great," she said. "I pop up a batch, then put it in that plastic container. It makes a marvelous cereal. Want to try it?"

"No, thanks, I'll pass." He poured himself some coffee, then sat opposite her at the table. He leaned slightly forward and peered into her bowl. "That really looks gross."

"Well, it's not. The trick is to remember not to salt it when you pop it."

Tyson chuckled and leaned back, tilting the chair onto two legs as he wrapped both hands around the mug of steaming coffee.

"So, tell me, Tyson," Sophie said pleasantly, "have you just not gotten around to discussing what happened between us last night, or do you have a set policy to avoid the topic on the morning after?"

Tyson choked on a swallow of coffee, and the legs of the chair thudded back onto the floor. He coughed, then glared at Sophie.

She plunked one elbow on the table and rested her chin in the palm of her hand, her eyebrows raised in a questioning manner.

"I'm going to pretend," Tyson said stiffly, "that you didn't ask that."

"Why?"

"Because," he said, getting to his feet, "I don't want to talk about it."

"Okay," she said in a singsong voice. She shoveled in another mouthful of popcorn.

"Oh, man," Tyson said, then strode away.

Very interesting, Sophie mused. Tyson was *still* shook up. However, the fact that he refused to discuss their lovemaking could very well mean that he didn't intend to repeat the experience. That would never do. She would simply have to change his mind.

Sophie was smiling as she rinsed the dishes and put them in the dishwasher. Back in her bedroom, she freshened her lipstick. When she emerged again, Tyson glanced over at her, then did a quick double take. She was wearing a fleece-lined bomber jacket of soft leather the same shade as her boots. Flung jauntily around her neck was a long, fringed, white silk scarf.

The lady didn't play fair, Tyson decided. The coiling heat low in his body gave evidence to the fact that the final additions to her ensemble were more than his raging libido could handle.

"Let's go," he said, then spun on his heel and headed for the door.

"Tyson, wait a minute," Sophie said, suddenly very serious.

He stopped and turned to look at her. "Yes? Hey, what is it, what's wrong?"

"You haven't said one word about the possibility of Jasco searching my home and business for the microdot. I know there's an agent out there watching the place, but Jasco managed to put that awful flower by the door and . . ." Her voice trailed off.

"Don't worry about him breaking in here, Sophie. He's pushing, taunting, but he wouldn't risk spending that much time in one place. He knows, we know, that it's useless to search a large area for a microdot. The chances of finding it are slim to none. No, he'll stick to the theory that *you* are aware of exactly where it is."

"That," Sophie said, "is not a particularly comforting thought."

"It should be. Remember, he has to go through me to get to you, and that isn't going to happen. Are you ready to leave?"

Sophie sighed, nodded, picked up her purse and followed Tyson out the door.

The day was clear with a bright sun that caused the snow to glisten and glitter like precious gems. The air was bitingly cold, creating a nearly burning sensation in lungs when a deep breath was drawn.

Sophie shuffled from one booted foot to the other in an attempt to keep warm as Tyson carefully inspected both of their vehicles.

"Well," Sophie said, her teeth chattering, "if Jasco didn't realize before that you're an agent, he certainly knows it now."

"He knew," Tyson said. "Okay, the cars are clean."

"Too late. My feet are frozen to the ground."

"Sophie, get in the car."

"Right."

The minute that Tyson started to back out of the driveway, Sophie began fiddling with the buttons on the dashboard.

"Heater," she said.

"Give it a few minutes."

"I'm placing my order," she said, then sank back against the plush seat.

"Where am I heading here?"

"Oh, take the Adlai Stevenson Expressway out of the city, then pick up I-55. Turn right at the next corner to get on LaSalle, drive through the business district to the Adlai Stevenson."

"Got it."

They fell silent, each lost in their own thoughts.

Sophie's mind echoed what Tyson had said several times about Jasco having to go through him to get to her.

Darn it, she thought. She didn't want him to place himself in danger because of her. *She did not want anything to happen to Tyson MacDonald.* He had no family, no one, but he wasn't alone—not anymore. *She* was there.

She snapped her head around to look at him. "Don't you dare get killed because of me, Tyson MacDonald," she blurted out, then shook her head in self-disgust as she realized what she'd said.

He glanced over at her, then redirected his attention to the traffic.

"Okay, Sophie," he said, smiling. "I won't get killed. I really wasn't planning on it, anyway."

"Of course you're not planning on it," she said crossly, "but you're setting yourself up for it. You're parading around in full view, and you intend to stand between Jasco and me if need be."

He shrugged. "I *am* trained for this type of thing, you know. Why are you getting upset about this now?"

"Because I... Just because, damn it," she said, nearly shrieking.

Tyson blinked in surprise at her outburst. "Oh. Look, trust me. Okay?"

"I do. I do trust you, Tyson."

"Then we're going to do just fine."

He looked over at her again, then back to the road.

But in that flicker of time when their eyes had met, it was as though they'd spoken at great length. Desire was transmitted, and caring, and something else that was potent, strong, which neither wished to examine further or give a name to. The sensuality in the close quarters of the vehicle seemed to weave and crackle through the air.

"Tyson," Sophie said, determined to break the spell that had been cast over them once again, "tell me about your childhood. It's very evident that you're a private person who doesn't like to talk about himself, but would you mind telling me? If you don't want to, I'll understand and respect that."

Tyson didn't speak for several minutes, and Sophie watched him intently.

Please, Tyson, she mentally pleaded. His sharing his most personal facts with her was important, meant so very much to her.

He cleared his throat, then finally spoke. "I never knew my parents," he said quietly. "I have no idea who they were. I was left in a church in New Jersey when I was a few weeks old and raised for several years in an orphanage. Later I moved from foster home to foster home."

"Oh, dear, I'm so sorry. Couldn't you have been adopted by a couple who wanted a child?"

"Yeah, I suppose, but it never happened. I went out on my own as soon as I could and joined the army. Being in the service gave me the first sense of belonging, of purpose, that I'd ever had.

"What I didn't realize during the time I was in the army was that I was being observed, evaluated by the agency. The fact that I had no ties, no one who was waiting for me to come home, combined with how I conducted myself, added up to what they were looking for. I was recruited, met your father about ten years ago, and the rest is history. It's not a very exciting tale. In fact, it's boring as hell."

"No, it isn't. Thank you for telling me, Tyson," Sophie said softly. "I know you don't want to hear again that I'm sorry you had a childhood like that, but I have to say it. Hank and I had so much, and it just doesn't seem fair that you had so little. Life isn't always fair."

"No."

"Who named you?"

"The headmistress of the orphanage, who was one hundred percent Scottish. It wasn't like in the movies where there's a note pinned to the kid's blanket saying who he is and please take good care of him. I was just left there. End of story."

"Sad story."

Tyson shrugged again.

"Have you thought about what you want to do when you decide to leave the agency?" Sophie said.

"I'm giving serious thought to quitting," he said, his hands tightening on the steering wheel. "I've been heading toward it, feeling the beginning of burnout."

"Oh?" Sophie said, feeling the increased tempo of her heart. "And if you *did* quit? What then?"

"I don't know. I could be a private investigator, or some kind of security systems expert, or whatever. I'm not sitting behind a desk for eight hours a day, that's for sure."

"No, I can't see you doing that," she said absently. He might quit, walk away from the dark side of life? Sophie Clarkson, stop it. She'd do well to zero in on the word *might.*

"I'll figure it all out later," Tyson said.

"Where do you think you'd like to live?" Sophie asked. Chicago? Well, it was none of her business. She was simply chatting now, getting to know Tyson better. But why couldn't he just open his mouth and say the word *Chicago?* "Never mind. You probably haven't given it all that much thought yet."

"No, I haven't because I haven't decided for certain if I'm going to quit."

"Where do you live now? I mean, you said you didn't have anything to decorate, but you must have a home port or whatever you want to call it."

"I have a furnished apartment in Los Angeles, but I'm not there much. I'd like—" he paused "—I'd like to have a house someday. You know, with a yard, trees, grass to mow. And a dog. I'll get him at the pound, a mangy mutt no one else wanted. I'll call him Buddy, because that's what we'd be . . . good friends, buddies." He stopped speaking and cleared his throat. "Who put a nickel in me? I don't ever run off at the mouth like this. Aren't we due to turn off the highway soon?"

Sudden and very unexpected tears misted Sophie's eyes. She quickly turned her head to look out the side window, hardly registering what was within her view.

"It's about two more miles," she said. "Take the Wheatville exit."

"Okay."

Oh, Tyson, Sophie thought, blinking away her tears. She could picture so clearly in her mind the lonely little boy he must have been, then the adolescent who turned his emotions inward, built the wall around himself for protection. He'd moved into adulthood alone, never having known the warmth and love of a family.

But slowly, slowly, he was revealing himself to her, trusting her, sharing, letting down his guard for her so that she could go past the wall. She wanted to reach out to him, hold him, tell him he wasn't alone anymore because she was there, they were together. Because...

Because she was in love with Tyson MacDonald?

Oh, no, she mustn't ask herself that question, as the answer was...

"Tyson's attic," she said, turning her head to look at him again.

"What?"

"Don't you see, Tyson? You *do* have a Tyson's attic where you've tucked away your dreams. A house with a yard, trees, grass to mow and Buddy. All those things are in your heart."

"Yeah, well..." He shifted in his seat as though he was no longer comfortable sitting there. "Whatever. There's the exit."

A gentle smile touched Sophie's lips as they left the highway and drove along a muddy, dirt road.

The barn where the auction was being held was large and painted traditional burnt red with white trim. Cars and pickup trucks were parked in a roped-off area, and people were milling around. Despite the biting cold, teenagers manned tables selling coffee, doughnuts, homemade bread and cookies.

Sophie and Tyson each had coffee and a doughnut, then went into the pleasant warmth of the barn. The center section held rows of folding metal chairs. Against the walls were a multitude of items, each having a yellow card with a number attached to it.

"Man, what a bunch of stuff," Tyson said. "How do you keep it all straight in your mind?"

"Practice, my dear," Sophie said cheerfully. "Lots of practice."

As they strolled along, Tyson kept silent as Sophie concentrated on the things to be auctioned. Tyson's eyes darted over the people gathered in the big building.

Was Jasco there? he wondered. Wearing some kind of disguise, was the sleazeball actually in that building, perhaps only a matter of a few feet away?

"Oh, fantastic," Sophie said.

Tyson turned and saw her peering closely at a weather-beaten wooden butter churn.

"Look at this, Tyson," she said, her blue eyes sparkling. "Isn't it wonderful?"

"It could use a coat of paint."

Sophie laughed. "Somehow I don't think you appreciate the artistic appearance of antiques. This is very valuable, and perfect for my client's country kitchen."

"What is she going to use it for?"

"Well, nothing. It's part of the decor. It will lend atmosphere, authenticity, to the room."

Tyson chuckled. "I still think a coat of paint would do wonders for the thing."

Sophie slipped her arm through his as they walked on down the row.

"You're hopeless," she said, smiling. "You should pay close attention to my lecture on Thursday night. You'll learn a thing or two about antiques. Oh, look there—a spinning wheel.''

Sophie slipped her arm free of Tyson's and hurried forward. He followed her at a leisurely pace.

Sophie's enthusiasm was infectious, he mused. It was hard to keep from smiling when she was bubbling with excitement. It was also impossible not to feel her pain when she was crying. The magic, as well as the sensual spell she continually cast over him, was growing stronger and stronger.

Lord, he thought, he couldn't believe he'd actually told her about his dream to someday have a house, and... What kind of jerk spilled his guts about wanting to have grass to mow? He'd even told her about Buddy.

He was really losing it, Tyson thought. He'd opened his big mouth and told Sophie things that no one else knew, not even Hank. Things that were personal, private, his, had been tucked away...

Yes! Tucked away in Tyson's attic!

He stopped in his tracks so suddenly that the person behind him bumped into him and mumbled apologies. Tyson quickened his step to catch up with Sophie, unable to hide the smile on his face.

Eight

At precisely eleven o'clock, a woman at the far end of the barn rang an old-fashioned brass bell, swinging her arm up and down as though announcing to children that school was about to begin.

The calm atmosphere in the barn immediately changed to one of buzzing excitement and enthusiasm. Everyone scurried to find places on the folding chairs. As Sophie started down the middle walkway, Tyson placed one hand on her arm to stop her. She looked up at him questioningly.

"Let's sit near the back," he said.

"Why?"

"Humor me."

"Whatever," she said, throwing up her hands.

They settled in the third row from the last, Sophie one chair in, Tyson on the center aisle. He slowly scrutinized the crowd, a blank expression on his face.

Two men at the front and two at the rear started down the middle aisle, passing out cards to those who wished them. They wrote down the recipient's name and the number of the card on paper attached to a clipboard. The white cardboard cards were six by nine inches, and the number on each was done in large black print.

Sophie received number eight.

"Now what?" Tyson said.

"This is my bidding number," she said. "We don't have to scream and yell. If I agree to the amount the auctioneer is asking for, I simply hold up my card. At some point, no one will respond to the new price, and the last price will stay. The woman at the front table will write down the bidder's number, the sum and the number of the item that was sold."

Tyson nodded. "Very organized."

"It's fun."

"What are you going after?"

"The butter churn, spinning wheel, a pitcher and washbowl and a set of four framed country prints."

"Sophie, we came in a car, not a moving van."

She laughed. "I'll make arrangements for delivery. There's the auctioneer. Here we go."

Within ten minutes, Tyson was shaking his head in wonder. He had not yet, he realized, understood more than one or two of the words the jabbering man at the front of the barn had said. The white cards popped up, were pointed to by the auctioneer as he called out the number on the card, then he continued on with his rapid-fire spiel.

It was fascinating, Tyson admitted to himself, albeit mystifying. The best part, however, was the enthralled expression on Sophie's face and her sparkling, dancing blue eyes.

Sold! The beautiful woman in the snazzy bomber jacket goes to the beat-up secret agent ... forever.

Forever? his mind echoed. If there was one thing he never dealt in, never gave thought to, it was the future in terms of forever. In his line of work, the future was contained in neat little packages that held nothing more than the successful completion of the current assignment.

No, he'd never dwelled on the tomorrows and what they might bring. Never ... until now, until Sophie. But the wayward path his mind was traveling down shouldn't surprise him at this point, not when he considered the fact that he'd gone so far as to tell Sophie about an imaginary mangy dog named Buddy.

"Darn it," Sophie said, bringing Tyson from his thoughts.

"What's wrong?" he said.

"I lost out on the butter churn. I've set limits for each of the items I want so that I'm certain that I stay within my client's budget."

Tyson patted her knee. "Count your blessings. Now you don't have to paint the thing."

"Oh, hush," she said, laughing. "You have an attitude problem."

Tyson chuckled, then they directed their attention to the front again as a set of huge, ornate lamps were presented to the crowd.

"Ugh," Sophie said.

"Ditto."

Jasco resisted the urge to cackle with glee as he saw the butter churn being moved to the area designated for items sold.

Fools, he thought. Miss High-and-Mighty Clarkson and her lover agent, MacDonald, couldn't beat him. Not at anything. He was Jasco. The idiots, idiots, idiots, hadn't seen him following them during the drive up here because he was superior, an unstoppable force.

He would make certain that Hank's Sophie didn't get any of the toys she wanted in this silly game they were playing with their childish numbered cards. She had number eight. He had thirteen, a lucky number this day as he snatched away what she coveted.

Jasco stroked the beard that was part of his disguise, his hand trembling as he envisioned the scar beneath, which was now nearly totally covered.

He deserved this time he'd allotted himself, he thought. Time to terrorize Sophie, time to frustrate MacDonald. Oh, yes, this was his due, a minute payback for what had been done to his face by Hank Clarkson.

But soon, very soon now, he must put his own pleasure aside and get the microdot from Sophie. She had it, of course. MacDonald had come, verifying that and was staying close to Sophie with the hope of catching him, the best, Jasco, when he came for it. They wouldn't even have had enough sense to place the microdot in government hands. Not them, not the fools. Oh, yes, Sophie had it.

He'd had his revenge against Hank Clarkson. Now Sophie was next. He'd get the microdot from her, then finish it once and for all. Sophie Clarkson would be dead, too.

Again Jasco had to control the laughter that bubbled in his throat.

Soon he would laugh, he thought. Soon he would laugh at the fools.

Over an hour later, Sophie sighed and shook her head. "I've never been beaten out like this before," she said.

"I don't always get everything I'm after, but this is ridiculous. The butter churn, pitcher and bowl and the prints went for more than I could justify spending."

"Well, you've still got a shot at the spinning wheel," Tyson said. "They're carrying it forward now. It must be next after that mirror. That is one ugly mirror. Who would want a mirror framed with plastic fruit?"

"Quite a few people, according to the way the bidding is going. Oh, I hope I get the spinning wheel."

Ten minutes later, the bidding began on the spinning wheel. Sophie sat on the edge of her chair, thrusting her card in the air time and again as the price went up at a furious pace.

"Well, damn," she muttered finally, sinking back in her seat. "It went over my limit...again. Whoever number thirteen is, he or she has money to burn. I can't tell from here's who's holding the card, but it's not bringing typical number-thirteen bad luck to whoever it is."

"Lost out to number thirteen, huh?" Tyson said. "Well, be nice. Maybe thirteen has yearned for a spinning wheel from the day he, she, whoever, was born."

"I don't feel like being nice," Sophie said, smiling despite herself. "That crummy thirteen beat me out on everything. All the items I was after went to thirteen."

Tyson stiffened, every muscle in his body tightening. "Isn't that rather unusual? You know, for one person to consistently outbid you?"

Sophie shrugged. "It's never happened before, but they were all for a country motif so it's certainly reasonable. I paid attention—thirteen didn't bid on anything else. There were other country pieces, but they didn't seem to be of interest. Oh, well, win some, lose some."

Tyson narrowed his eyes as he felt a familiar prickly sensation at the back of his neck.

Maybe, just maybe, he thought, his eyes darting over the crowd. Jasco. Yeah, Jasco would like this. He'd get a rush out of depriving Sophie of what she wanted. He'd be continuing his cat-and-mouse game before making his final move toward Sophie for the microdot.

"Sophie," Tyson said quietly, "what happens after the last item is sold?"

"The people who bought things go to the table at the front there to pay, then move to the next table if they want to make delivery arrangements."

"What if someone changes their mind? He thought it over and decided he didn't want what he'd won the bid on?"

"There's no record of who was runner-up, so to speak. The item would be held over for the next auction. That doesn't happen often, but once in a while someone just walks out without their goodies."

Tyson nodded. "Okay. Where did you see this number-thirteen card being raised?"

"Way over there near the left front, about two or three rows back from the side entrance and close to the aisle." She frowned. "Why? What are all these questions leading up to?"

"Maybe something, maybe nothing."

Sophie's eyes widened. "Tyson, are you suggesting that number thirteen is Jasco? Here?"

"It fits, Sophie. Think about it. The whole program would appeal to his sick mind. You stay here. I'm going over to where you saw the thirteen. Don't move. Understand?"

"Yes, but—"

"Ah, damn," he said. "I waited too long."

The auction was over, and the people were rising en masse, spilling out into the aisles, the noise level once again on high.

"Don't move," Tyson repeated.

He got to his feet and started forward, muttering his apologies as he went. He felt like a salmon swimming upstream as he forced his way through the crowd that was going in the opposite direction. Frustration and fury caused him to clench his jaw until it ached.

By the time Tyson reached the far side of the building, the chairs were empty. He hurried to the table where a line had formed, comprised of those who had purchases to pay for. He scanned the people, seeing no one who even slightly resembled Jasco.

How good at disguises was the creep? Tyson wondered. Oh, hell, who was he kidding? He'd bet his last dime that number thirteen wouldn't claim the items he'd won. Jasco was long gone out that side door. Guaranteed.

"Tyson?"

He snapped his head around and glared at Sophie. "I told you to stay put."

"And I did . . . for a while."

"Yeah, well, it doesn't matter now. If he was here, he's gone. Lord, I can't believe I was so slow on the uptake. I should have been paying closer attention to who was outbidding you."

"Don't be so hard on yourself. You had no way of knowing that . . ."

"There's no excuse for my sloppy work, Sophie. I blew it, pure and simple. I'll check once these people in line have settled up. Ten will get you twenty that number thirteen won't have claimed his stuff. You realize, don't you, that I completely missed the fact that Jasco was tailing us? He had to have followed us up here."

"Well . . ."

Tyson laughed, a short, humorless bark of sound. "Man, I'm great at my job, aren't I? A green rookie would have done better than this."

"Stop it, Tyson," Sophie said. "I'm not blaming you, so lighten up. Besides, you don't know for certain that Jasco was here."

"If the antiques are left unclaimed, Jasco was here."

Number thirteen did not pay for his purchases.

Outside, Tyson let out a pent-up breath and stared up at the sky for a long moment.

"Don't worry," he said, looking at Sophie. "I'm not going to bite your head off all the way back into town. My lousy performance is my problem. Do be assured, though, that it won't happen again. I'm not going to let my guard down for a second."

"Fine," Sophie said, smiling. "Are you ready to go? I don't know about you, but I'm hungry. There's a family restaurant near here that has delicious home cooking and pies I'd sell my soul for. I refuse to get upset about what took place here, Tyson. You're stressed out enough for both of us."

Tyson laughed and shook his head. He slid one arm across her shoulders and pulled her close to his side. Sophie shivered with delight. "Lead me to the homemade pies."

She refused to dwell on the fact that Jasco had actually been in the auction barn, Sophie decided as they walked to the car. It was terrifying to realize that he would run such risks of being caught simply to cause her upset and disappointment over not obtaining the items she wanted. Tyson would, no doubt, stew enough for a dozen people about the episode.

During lunch, Sophie chattered on about past victories at auctions, as well as defeats. She related the humorous story of being given a card with the number six, had thought it was a nine, and completely fouled up the record keeping.

Tyson laughed in appreciation of the hilarious tale of a mix-up in delivery, which had resulted in an erotic, life-size marble statue being delivered to a church rectory, while a child's frilly canopy bed arrived at a bemused playboy's penthouse apartment.

The remaining drive back into the city was quiet, due to the fact that sleet was now falling in torrents. Tyson's total concentration was directed at the barely visible road ahead.

"Man, it's slow going," Tyson said. "At this rate, it'll take us nearly twice as long to get back as it did coming."

"No problem," Sophie said. Except for the fact that she was liable to leap across the seat and start tearing Tyson's clothes off his body. She kept her thoughts to herself, saying instead, "We'll fix dinner at the house. If we stop at a restaurant, we'll run the risk of the roads being worse than they are now. We can eat in front of the fire."

Tyson chuckled. "And you can take off your shoes. Well, boots in this case."

"Yes," she said. Step by step, inch by emotional inch, without even wishing to or being aware of it, Tyson was spinning silken threads around her heart, mind, the very essence of her being.

And before he left, she wanted, needed, to tuck safely into the attic of her heart many more memories of joining her body with his, making love with Tyson, becoming one.

"Oh, my," Sophie said with a soft sigh.

"That was a strange-sounding sigh," Tyson said. "Was it boredom, fatigue, hunger?"

Try desire, MacDonald, she thought, stifling laughter. Try good old, earthy, sensual desire.

"None of the above," she said. "Well, we're almost home. At least the sleet has stopped. I imagine it's bitter cold out there, though."

"No doubt about it."

At long last Tyson turned into the driveway at Sophie's. Darkness had fallen with a heavy curtain, the snow-laden clouds not allowing even the most insistent stars to twinkle in the inky sky. He frowned as he turned off the ignition.

"It's dark as pitch," he said. "Let's lock the car, then I'll go up the stairs first. Stay close behind me."

"Wait a minute," Sophie said, rummaging through her purse. "I have one of those pen flashlights. It's not great, but you'll at least be able to find the keyhole. Here it is." She handed it to Tyson.

After the car was securely locked, Tyson hurried up the stairs with Sophie right behind him. He held the house key at the ready.

At the top of the small porch, they stopped, a gasp escaping from Sophie's lips as Tyson shone the light on the door.

"Oh, dear God," she whispered.

Rage rushed through Tyson like a wild current, causing a red haze to blur his vision for a moment.

"Tyson?" Sophie said, grasping one of his arms.

"Damn him," he said, a pulse beating wildly in his temple.

"That knife..." Sophie said, her voice trembling. "That...knife is embedded in my door. It looks so evil, so..."

Tyson handed Sophie the flashlight, then took a handkerchief from his pocket and, touching as little of the knife as possible, he eased it out of the wood panel.

"I'll have this checked for fingerprints, but there's no doubt in my mind who put it there."

"Jasco," Sophie whispered.

"Yeah. He went out the side door at the auction barn and hightailed it back here. It's so dark that my man never saw him approach the house. Jasco is really getting cocky, very bold, which makes him all that more dangerous. Enough is enough."

"What do you mean?"

"It's time to end it. I'm going to force Jasco's hand."

Nine

Sophie had to actually give her feet firm mental directives to move one after the other to enable her to follow Tyson into the house.

It was just too much, she thought hazily. She'd managed to ignore the realization that Jasco had been in the auction barn, had shoved that fact into a dusty corner of her mind and left it there.

But, dear Lord, now there was that hideous knife. The events at the auction suddenly refused to stay where she'd placed them. They had emerged front row center to combine with that ugly, evil-looking knife, and she had nowhere to put it all. It was just too, too much.

Tyson locked the door, set the handkerchief containing the knife on an end table, snapped on a light, then shrugged out of his jacket. He draped the jacket over the back of a chair, then checked the other rooms. When he returned, he saw that Sophie hadn't moved from where she stood next to the door.

"Sophie," he said, closing the distance between them, "take off your jacket. I'll hang it in the closet for you."

She looked at him with a rather befuddled expression. "What?"

"Oh, man," he said under his breath.

"Take...off...I can't remember what you told me to do," she said, speaking very slowly. "I...don't...seem to be...able to think clearly..."

Tyson gripped her upper arms and gave her a small shake, causing her to stare up at him with wide eyes.

"Come on, Sophie, snap out of it," he said, not releasing his hold on her. "You've had a shock, but you're all right. I'm here, we're together and nothing is going to happen to you. Hey, I need you with me, partner. We've got a criminal to catch. We're going to get him, Sophie. We're going to get Jasco."

Sophie stared at Tyson for another long moment, then blinked, shook her head and blinked again.

"Damn him," she said finally. "He killed my father and now he's playing with me like I'm nothing more than an insect. Jasco is not going to get away with any of this."

Tyson looked up at the ceiling for a second and let out a pent-up breath. He met Sophie's gaze again.

"Welcome back," he said, managing a small smile. "You phased out on me there for a bit, scared me to death. Give me your jacket, then we have to talk."

"I'll tend to it," she said, unzipping the bomber jacket. She hung it in the closet, set her purse on the shelf, then sat in her favorite fan-backed chair. Within minutes her boots were off. "What do you want to talk about? Well, obviously it's regarding Jasco, but you're awfully serious. Are you hungry?"

"No." He crossed the room and began to prepare paper, kindling and logs for a fire. He lit a match, watched the paper begin to burn then ignite the kindling, before he rose and put the screen back into place. He turned to face Sophie, shoving his hands into his back pockets. "Sophie, I'm changing the rules."

"Meaning?"

"We're not partners in this anymore. I'm the protector, you're the protectee. What I'm trying to say is, you've been benched. You're sitting this out while I get the job done."

Sophie jumped to her feet, instantly wishing she still had the advantage of the two-inch heels on her fashion boots. She planted her fists on her hips and glared up at Tyson.

"I'm sitting on the bench?" she said none too quietly. "The hell I am, MacDonald. That was *my* father who was murdered, *my* front door that has a hole in it caused by the ugliest knife I've ever seen. You can give orders from here to Sunday, buster, but you'll be wasting your breath. We're in this together—us, two, a team—whether you like it or not."

Tyson yanked his hands out of his pockets and gripped her upper arms as he'd done before.

"Listen to me," he said. "Would you just listen to me for a minute? Jasco is sicker than I thought—he's totally lost it. The signs are there, Sophie. I've seen them before—I know what I'm talking about. He's taking enormous risks, seeing how close to the fire he can get without being burned."

"Well, big macho deal," Sophie said with an angry sniff. "That doesn't justify your telling me I'm supposed to sit in the corner now with my thumb in my mouth while you do your hero routine. Not a chance."

"You're not getting the picture here, Sophie," he said, the pulse in his temple beating wildly again. "Trust me, will you? If Hank were alive, he'd be drawing the same conclusions about Jasco that I am. Jasco intends to kill you, Sophie—"

"I know that!"

"And he doesn't care if he dies while he's doing it," Tyson shot back.

Sophie opened her mouth to retort, then snapped it closed again as the impact of Tyson's words made her suddenly short of breath.

Tyson shifted his hands from her arms to her face, cradling her soft skin in his callus-roughened hands. His voice was pitched low and was quiet when he finally spoke again.

"Jasco is dangerous, Sophie," he said. "He's far more dangerous than he was years ago. I can't let you be in harm's way, I just can't. If something happened to you, I wouldn't... Ah, hell, Sophie, I don't know what I'd do if...damn!"

Then his mouth came down hard onto hers.

Sophie's eyes flew wide open in shock at the unexpected and rough onslaught of Tyson's lips. But in the next instant, the kiss gentled and Sophie's lashes slowly drifted down. Her hands moved to encircle his neck as his hands dropped from her face and splayed on her back. He urged her closer, and she complied, nestling her softness next to his rugged length, feeling his arousal pressing heavily against her.

Sophie savored the taste of Tyson, along with his aroma of soap, winter air and man. She inched her fingers into his thick hair, felt the sweet pain of her breasts being crushed to the hard wall of his chest. Heat swirled within her, thrumming low with an increasing pulse.

Oh, yes, Tyson, her mind hummed. This night, they would again be one, make love, exquisite love, that would be a precious, treasured memory to tuck into the attic of her heart.

Tyson drew a sharp breath, then his mouth claimed Sophie's once again. He parted her lips, his tongue delving into the darkness. She met his tongue eagerly with her own, touching, stroking in a seductive ritual that caused their desire to soar.

Nothing, Sophie vowed hazily, would be allowed to intrude on the splendor of this night. The threat of danger beyond the door, the insane man bent on revenge, the chilling fear of what Jasco might do next, the lingering sorrow and anger over Hank's senseless death...none of it, *nothing,* would dim the wondrous glow. This was their world, and there was only room for the two of them.

Tyson tore his mouth from Sophie's and clenched his jaw as he strove to regain control, to quell the flame of passion that burned within him.

Sophie slowly opened her eyes, and a groan rumbled in his chest as he saw the desire in the smoky blue depths, desire he knew she could read in his eyes, as well. Her lips were moist and slightly parted, inviting, tempting, calling to him to claim them with his own.

He ached with a want and need so intense that the blood pounded in his veins and his heart beat with a wild, painful cadence.

And with the physical desire of Sophie came the emotions. He forced his mind to skitter past the one emotion that lingered in the shadows, refusing to acknowledge it or seek its name.

He had to step away from Sophie...now.

He had to break the sensual spell...now.

She'd changed his life already, and the risk of going further was too great.

He couldn't have, he knew, what was far beyond his reach. Sophie walked in a circle of sunshine. He was rough edged, earthy, raw. And he walked alone in the darkness of death.

"I want you, Tyson," Sophie whispered, close to his lips.

"Oh, Sophie, don't," he said, his voice gritty with passion. He pulled her hands from his neck, then held her splayed fingers against his chest. "No. No, I'm not going to make love with you."

"Why are you refusing me, Tyson? I know you were troubled after our lovemaking, that you regretted what had taken place, but I don't know why."

He shook his head, then took a step backward, releasing her hands and forcing her to drop them from his chest.

"I want to make love with you, Tyson MacDonald," Sophie said. "There it is...as honest and real as it can be. I want you very, very much."

Tyson dragged a restless hand through his hair. "Don't say it again. I'm hanging on by a thread here. Don't push me, Sophie. I want you so damn much. No."

"No?" Sophie repeated, then wrapped her hands around her elbows in a protective gesture. "Well, that's certainly clear enough, isn't it? There's no big mystery about why—you simply don't want to make love with me. You could have softened the rejection a bit, but that wouldn't be your style, would it, Tyson? You're a 'tell it like it is' man, up-front, no-holds-barred. You want me...but no."

"Sophie—"

"My, aren't we the epitome of a modern-day couple?" she went on, attempting a smile that failed. "We have a classic case of role reversal here. I, the woman, am trying to get you to let me ravish your body. You, the man, are standing firm, saying no. What are you protecting, Tyson? Your virtue? That, of course, is absurd. My pride is already in shreds, so you might as well tell me. Yes, let's go back to the question of why, after all. I asked you to make love to me, and you refused. Why? Why, Tyson?" Sudden tears misted her eyes. "Damn you, Tyson MacDonald, why?"

"Because you scare the hell out of me, lady," he said none too quietly. "Because I want you *too* much, if you can even begin to understand that. Because I told you about Buddy the dog, and mowing the grass, and...because I've never felt like this before, and I don't like it. I have no intention of figuring out what is happening here and... Ah, hell, forget it."

And Sophie Clarkson smiled.

It was a gentle smile, a womanly smile, a smile of wisdom and understanding. It was a smile of wondrous joy because she knew that Tyson MacDonald cared very deeply for her, although he'd probably deny it with his last breath. It was a smile that wrapped itself around that precious moment in time, and she carefully tucked the memory into the attic of her heart.

It was a smile that was Tyson's undoing as Sophie lifted one hand, palm up, in his direction.

"This is our night, Tyson," she said quietly, "if you want it to be. No commitments, no promises, no regrets. I *will* say it again. I want to make love with you, Tyson MacDonald."

He stared up at the ceiling for a long moment, the gesture one that was now very familiar and uniquely his,

Sophie realized. She waited, her hand held out toward him, steady, with not even a trace of trembling evident.

Tyson was warring with himself, she knew, and all she could do was wait to discover whether his mind or his heart had the strongest voice.

He met her gaze again, looked at her hand, then back into her eyes.

"I have nothing to offer you, Sophie," he said, his voice low and rough.

"I'm not asking for anything except you and this night—our night."

He nodded, then raised one hand and grasped hers, his large hand nearly eclipsing her smaller one. He dropped her hand in the next moment, wove his fingers into the silken, wavy depths of her strawberry blond hair and closed the short distance separating them. He visually traced each of her features, his smoldering gaze finally coming to rest on her lips.

As he covered her mouth with his, he knew he was lost, gone, would not be able to step away and regain control. He was going to make love with Sophie once again, and the mere image in his mind of what they would share caused his blood to thunder and his manhood to surge with the want of her.

He allowed the emotion free rein, but still skittered over the one that had no name. The possessiveness was there, and with it came the message that Sophie was his. With the future encompassing no more than the next beat of his racing heart, beautiful Sophie was his.

Tyson, Sophie thought. She moved the sound of his name through the chambers of her mind, heart, the very essence of her soul. On this night, this private, stolen night, he would be hers once more, sharing the most intimate act known to woman and man.

The kiss ended, another followed, and yet another. Then by unspoken agreement they went across the room and into the bedroom. The light from the living room cast a faint rosy glow over the room, creating a nearly ethereal aura.

The spread on the double bed was a pattern of daisies, like a field of the enchanting flower. The dresser and end tables were white; a small easy chair was mint green. Sophie swept back the blankets to reveal mint green sheets, then turned to gaze at Tyson. He looked directly into her eyes for a long moment, then reached for the waistband of his sweater.

"No, wait," Sophie said, her voice hushed. "Please. Just stand there for now, all right?"

Tyson nodded, but his brows knitted in a slight frown of confusion. A few seconds later, the frown disappeared and was replaced by an expression of smoldering desire as Sophie began to slowly, so slowly, unbutton her blouse.

She shifted the silky material below her shoulders, then allowed it to slither to the floor in an emerald-colored pool. Her lacy bra followed, the glow of light casting its rosy hue over the creamy skin of her lush, bare breasts.

Tyson's arousal strained against the zipper of his jeans, and he curled his hands into tight fists at his sides. He forced himself not to move, not to reach out and haul Sophie into his arms.

She had asked him to wait, and he would, somehow. But, oh, she was so exquisite, and he wanted her so much he was about to explode.

As Sophie unzipped her jeans then inched them down, catching her bikini panties with her thumbs as she went, a groan rumbled in Tyson's chest.

This was, he thought in a passion-laden haze, the most sensual, erotic scene he had ever witnessed. And it was more than that, too. Sophie was rendering herself vulnerable, was about to be naked before him, open to his scrutiny while he remained fully dressed.

What trust she had in him, he marveled. What an incredible gift she was offering him at that very moment, a moment that would be placed in Tyson's attic in his heart just the way Sophie had taught him.

And he burned. He was on fire with the want of her as his gaze visually traced every inch of her dewy skin. She was femininity personified. She was his.

Sophie stepped forward and outlined Tyson's lips with the tip of her tongue. A shudder ripped through him, and he started to raise his arms to encircle her.

"No," she whispered. "Wait."

"Sophie, I . . ." he began, his voice gritty.

"Shh. Just wait."

Sophie worked Tyson's sweater upward, and he raised his arms so she could draw it over his head as she stood on tiptoe to accomplish her task. With a featherlike touch of her fingertips, she made it clear that she wished Tyson to once again drop his arms to his sides. He complied while aware of the racing tempo of his heart.

Sophie slid her hands through the dark curls on Tyson's chest, feeling his muscles tense beneath her foray. She explored every inch of his chest, her hands never still, her fingers instruments of sweet torture as she found his nipples, teased, tantalized, then moved on.

And then where her hands had been, her lips followed.

Tyson closed his eyes for a moment, drawing on willpower, his hands once again tight fists at his sides.

Sophie's tongue flickered here, there, everywhere, tasting the salty flavor of Tyson's damp skin. She savored his aroma and the feel of his taut, quivering muscles. Without stopping her exploration, her hands reached for the snap on his jeans, then slid down the zipper.

She worked the faded fabric over his lean hips and caught his briefs with her thumbs as she'd done with her panties.

She moved in tandem with the clothing...lower...lower...her lips caressing, nibbling, paying homage to all that came into her view.

"So...phie," Tyson said, hardly able to breathe. "It's heaven... You're giving...so much, but I can't hold on here...any longer."

She rose, smiled at him, then took one of his hands and urged him to the bed. With a sweep of her arm, she indicated that he should recline on the cool sheets. He lay before her, and her eyes swept over him, appreciating anew the magnificence of his glistening body.

Then she moved onto the bed and stretched out on top of him, covering his mouth with hers, plummeting her tongue within. Tyson groaned and wrapped his arms around her, crushing her breasts to his chest. The kiss deepened.

After a few minutes, Sophie raised her head and slid her hands to lie flat on his chest, pushing against his arms, which held her. He released her, watching her face, waiting to see what was next in a scenario that was definitely under Sophie's command.

She slowly straightened, her legs bent, knees on each side of Tyson's hips. She moved again and settled the dark, heated haven of her femininity over Tyson's aroused manhood.

...son said, his voice a hoarse whis-

She reached for his hands and placed them on her breasts. As Tyson began to stroke her, she rotated her hips to take him fully, completely within her.

"Love me, Tyson," she whispered. "I'm yours."

The rhythm began, perfectly synchronized, increasing in tempo until they were a thundering entity. Sophie threw her head back and called Tyson's name as he gripped her hips to hold her tightly against him.

The tension within Sophie coiled, built, growing stronger, tightening . . . tightening. . . .

"Tyson!"

He arched his back and thrust one more time, lifting them both above the bed, above reality, above any ecstasy they'd ever known.

"Sophie!"

Lingering spasms rippled through her, then she fell forward onto his chest, his arms automatically wrapping around her. Their rough breathing echoed in the quiet room.

Neither spoke. Their bodies began to cool, breathing returned to normal levels, and hearts beat in steady, natural rhythms. With his last ounce of energy, Tyson gently lifted Sophie off him, then tucked her close to his side. He pulled up the blankets. And still, neither spoke. The wonder of what they had shared was beyond words.

"I don't know what to say," Sophie finally said quietly. She wove her fingers through the curls on his chest. "It was so beautiful."

"Yes," Tyson said, his chin resting lightly on the top of her head. "It really was." They had made love again . . . it hadn't been just sex, physical release . . . they had made love. "Sophie?"

"Yes?"

"I..." He paused. "Are you all right? I didn't hurt you, did I?"

"Oh, no, not at all. I was the one who sort of... took charge. I'm most definitely all right, Tyson. There just aren't words to describe how I feel. I..." She yawned. "Oh, I'm sleepy, so contented and sleepy, like a kitten in a circle of sunshine. You should get a kitten when, well, if you ever get Buddy the dog, so he'll have someone to play with when you're not home."

"Yeah," he said, a slow, lazy quality to his voice, "a cat. Maybe I'll get one if I ever—I'll name it Soapy."

"Oh, gee whiz, golly," Sophie said, laughing softly, "I'm so honored."

"You should be. I don't name my cat after just anyone, you know."

"Indeed not." She yawned again.

"Go to sleep. I'll hold you just like this. Go to sleep, Sophie."

Would Tyson listen to his heart? she wondered as her eyes drifted closed. Would he surrender to his growing feelings for her? Or would he walk out of her life, leaving her to cry lonely tears in the night... forever?

Ten

Sophie slowly emerged from a cocoon of deep, dreamless sleep, hovering on the edge of consciousness, toying hazily with the urge to succumb once again to the delicious, warm depths of slumber.

But to awaken, her heart whispered insistently, was to see Tyson, touch Tyson, reach across the bed and feel the solid strength and vibrant heat of Tyson MacDonald. To awaken was to repeat in the light of the new day the wondrous rapture of their lovemaking shared during the darkness of night.

A soft smile formed on Sophie's lips, yet she still didn't open her eyes as she savored the sweet, sensuous memories in her mind. Time and again through the hours of the night, Tyson had reached for her—or had she sought him?—and they had become one entity, meshed, as they spiraled up and away and out of control, to be flung into glorious oblivion.

Sophie sighed in pure, feminine pleasure, then stretched like a lazy kitten. She turned her head on the pillow, a smile and Tyson's name on her lips, one hand lifting of its own volition toward him to connect.

But the expanse of bed next to Sophie was empty.

She sat bolt upward, clutching the sheet to her bare breasts as she listened, hardly breathing, for any sound in another room that would indicate that Tyson was there.

Silence.

She left the bed, slipped on her robe, which hung on a hook inside the closet door, and hurried out of the bedroom. In the living room, her eyes flew immediately to the end table where Tyson had placed the hideous knife. It was nowhere in sight.

A faint aroma of coffee reached her, and she went on to the kitchen. No Tyson. There was a freshly brewed pot of coffee, a mug in the sink and a note on the counter. She snatched up the paper, decided that Tyson should have been a doctor instead of a government agent and attempted to decipher the message.

"Well," she said aloud, smacking the note back onto the counter, "he has a lot of nerve."

With a frown firmly in place, she filled a mug with coffee, then went into the living room to sit in her favorite chair.

Tyson MacDonald, she fumed, has issued orders in his no-nonsense little missive like a Marine drill sergeant. He had gone out to make a telephone call. She was to stay in the house with the door locked, and was not to open the door to anyone.

"Yes, sir," she said. "Should I salute, too?"

Oh, cut it out, Sophie, she admonished herself. She was pouting like a child who hadn't been allowed to play in a game she was supposed to be a part of. But this *wasn't* a game—far from it, and Tyson knew, much better than she did, what action should be taken to apprehend Jasco.

Tyson had gone out to make a telephone call? she mentally repeated. She had a perfectly good phone that he could have used to... Oh, Lord, did he think Jasco had managed to tap her line, would be able to hear every word spoken during a call?

Sophie shivered, then took a sip of coffee.

She hated this, she thought. She really hated having her buttons pushed by an evil man like Jasco. He was forcing her to square off against cold reality when she would have chosen to remain, at least for a while longer, in the rosy, warm world that belonged only to her and Tyson.

Sophie sighed, decided that facts were facts and she might as well resign herself to that. There was a maniac out there who had murdered her father and was now determined to kill her.

But the one thing that Tyson MacDonald had better get straight in his mind was that she had no intention of being wrapped in protective cotton and placed on a shelf until this nightmare was over. Not a chance.

She had a second mug of coffee, showered, dressed in jeans and a green sweatshirt, then puttered around straightening up the house. She polished the furniture for a lack of anything better to do, vacuumed, put fresh linens on the bed and waited for Tyson.

And waited ... and waited ... and waited.

Tyson stood in the glass-enclosed booth, one hand gripping the black receiver of the telephone, the fingers of his other hand drumming an impatient rhythm on the tattered, graffiti-covered directory on the small shelf.

"There's no change at all in Hank's condition?" he asked. A deep frown knitted his dark brows. "None?"

"That's what I said," a man replied. "Hank is still in a coma. The doctors have nothing more to say at this point. It's all wait and see."

"Damn it, Leonard, do you have any idea how rough it is on Sophie to believe that her father is dead? She is *not* going to take kindly to the fact that I, we, lied to her about this. She has the right to at least see Hank, even if he wouldn't know she was there."

"*No,* absolutely not. We're not going to run the risk of leading Jasco straight to Hank. Jasco wouldn't rest until he'd finished the job of killing Hank. Jasco is too slick, too slippery. It's better this way. We have Hank under wraps, so we only have one Clarkson out there to protect . . . Sophie, and that's your problem."

"Well, I'm stepping up the tempo of this operation, Len. I want it wrapped up so that Sophie's out of harm's way *and* can be taken to see her father."

"If he's still alive by then."

"And if he isn't?"

"Then Sophie Clarkson will never be told that it wasn't her father in that sealed casket buried at the funeral."

Tyson muttered several earthy expletives.

"Swear all you want to, MacDonald," Leonard said, "just follow your orders." He paused. "So, you have the knife with you?"

"Yeah," Tyson said, squeezing the bridge of his nose. "I'm hoping that Jasco followed me away from Sophie's this morning. He should know by now that I didn't think the knife was important enough to meet with my man outside of the house and pass it on to him. That ought to fire up Jasco's temper. Guaranteed."

"Definitely. The more angry he gets increases the chances of his taking foolish risks. We want the knife as evidence, and your plan for tonight is sound. I'll set it up, then you go for it. But for God's sake, take care of Sophie. She's a private citizen and . . ."

"I'm well aware of that," Tyson interrupted gruffly. "You conveniently forget it whenever I say she has the right to know that her father is alive."

"Knock it off, MacDonald. That subject is officially closed for now."

"Yeah, right," Tyson said, shaking his head in disgust. "Put the wheels in motion for tonight." He slammed the receiver into place, not bothering to say goodbye.

The suits in charge, he fumed, had ice in their veins. Over the years, they'd lost any human quality they might have had. Would that happen to him in time? Not if he quit, got out now. But that wasn't the issue at the moment. He'd deal with all of that later.

He stepped out of the telephone booth and immediately hunched his shoulders against the bitingly cold wind that whipped along the street.

He also, he decided, wasn't going to dwell on the lovemaking shared with Sophie last night. All his lofty intentions to not touch her again had flown out the window. They'd been fantastic together. Incredible. Beautiful.

"Shut up, MacDonald," he said under his breath, "and get to work."

With his hands jammed into his jacket pockets, he strode down the sidewalk, mentally directing Jasco to follow close behind.

In the middle of the afternoon, Sophie ate a sandwich she really didn't want, then wandered back into the living room, wondering how on earth she was going to pass the time until Tyson returned.

What was taking him so long? she pondered. It surely didn't require hours to make a simple telephone call to heaven only knew whom. Oh, God, what if something had happened to Tyson? What if Jasco had been skulking around out there? What if Tyson was hurt? Or... No, she mustn't panic just because he'd been gone for an eternity.

She looked out the window for the umpteenth time, sighed, decided she was tired of hearing the oh-poor-me sound, then sighed again, anyway.

How dare Tyson subject her to this anxiety, she thought with a sudden burst of anger. He had no right to treat her in such a heartless, uncaring manner. A person who said he would be gone only long enough to make a telephone call, then had not reappeared hours later, was thoughtless, selfish, self-centered and rude.

When Tyson showed up, she mentally raged on as she flopped back into her chair, she was going to give him a piece of her mind, by gum—tell him exactly where he could put himself. Oh, yes, she would inform him in no uncertain words that because she was in love with him, he should be more considerate of her feelings.

She stiffened, her eyes widening.

"What?" she said. What? She was in love with Tyson? Oh, dear heaven, yes. She could no longer ignore the truth.

She was totally, absolutely, irrevocably in love with Tyson MacDonald.

She wanted to shout with joy, burst into song, fling herself into Tyson's arms when he returned and declare her undying love over and over.

She wanted to run as far and as fast as she could, putting as much distance as possible between herself and Tyson.

She wanted to rage at herself in fury for having succumbed to all that Tyson was as a man, causing her to lose her heart to him.

She wanted to weep in despair over the injustice of having waited so long to love, only to have chosen the wrong man.

She wanted to hold fast to the thread of hope that when the nightmare of knowing a murderer was after her was over, and Tyson stood at the crossroads of his life, he would take the path leading to the house, the trees, the grass to mow and Buddy the mangy mutt. He would reach out his hand to her, ask her to travel that road with him because he loved her, needed her, intended to stay by her side until death parted them.

She wanted . . . she wanted . . . she wanted . . . and it all was tumbling together in a jumbled maze of confusion in her weary mind.

Suddenly Sophie's tormented thoughts were interrupted and her head snapped around as she heard a noise at the door. Her eyes widened as she realized that a key was being turned in the lock.

No one had a key to the house, she thought, her heart and mind racing. She got up from the chair, ignored the trembling in her legs and grabbed the poker next to the fireplace.

In the next instant, the door opened, Sophie raised the poker high in the air and Tyson MacDonald entered the living room.

He closed the door, eyed the poker, then smiled.

"Practicing your golf swing?" he asked.

Sophie dropped the poker with no regard for the sooty marks it made on the carpeting and raced across the room. She flung her arms around Tyson's neck as she hurled against him, causing him to stagger slightly from the impact.

He wrapped one arm across her waist, his other hand being engaged in holding a hanger with one finger. Whatever was attached to the hanger was draped out of view down his back.

"Oh, Tyson," Sophie said, burying her face in the fleecy collar of his jacket. "I was so terribly worried about you. You were gone so long, I was afraid that Jasco had..."

"Hey," he said, "whoa, slow down. I'm sorry I upset you. I really am sorry. I just didn't think about what you might imagine had happened when I didn't come right back. I'm not used to having anyone who would care if I... But you *do* care, don't you? That's really something, Sophie. It's a little bit unsettling, too, I guess, but it's very nice."

"I'm glad you think so," she said, not moving. *Care?* It was far, far more than that. She was, heaven help her, in love with this man. "Oh, I'm so relieved to see you, I'm not even angry. I was really going to let you have it when you got back. Well, this is much better." She wiggled against him. "You feel good, smell good. MacDonald, you *are* good."

He chuckled. "You keep it up and I'll be demonstrating that fact in a few seconds. We have to talk, though, Sophie. Besides, if I don't hang this thing in the closet, my finger is going to fall off."

Sophie reluctantly lifted her head and moved slightly away from Tyson.

"Hang what thing in the closet?" she said, confusion evident on her face.

Tyson swung the hanger around and held it at arm's length, revealing a clear, thin plastic bag covering clothing.

"A tuxedo?" Sophie said. Her gaze swept over the garments encased in the bag. "Yes, that's a tuxedo, all right, with all the trimmings, and it looks like a very expensive one."

"Yep." Tyson crossed the room and hung the bag in the closet. He put his jacket on a hanger next to it. "Any coffee left?"

"Yes. Did you have lunch?"

"I grabbed a hamburger a couple of hours ago." He started toward the kitchen.

"Tyson, why do you have an expensive tuxedo hanging in the closet?"

"I'll explain everything," he called from the other room.

Sophie sat in her favorite chair and watched as Tyson crossed the room and settled onto the sofa. He took a sip of coffee from the mug he held, then nodded in approval.

"Hits the spot," he said. "I've been racing around ever since I left here."

"You're driving me nuts," Sophie said. "Would you tell me what's going on? I trust you've canceled your plan to bench me?"

"I'd like to keep you out of this from now on," he said, frowning, "but I don't have much choice in the matter."

"Why? Where have you been all these hours?"

"Okay, from the top. I went out to make a telephone call because I didn't want to run the risk of Jasco having tapped your line. I also wanted to give Jasco the impression that the knife was no big deal, so I didn't make contact with my man stationed outside. That will not sit well with our friend Jasco. I stayed very visible, and hope to hell that Jasco was tight on my tail."

He took another swallow of coffee, then shifted to pull Sophie's keys from his pocket.

"Let me give you these before I forget," he said, setting them on the end table. He stared at the worn key chain for a long moment. "I took them out of your purse. I assume you took dancing lessons when you were a little girl. That would account for the ballerina charm."

"No, I . . . Tyson, would you please get on with this?"

"Oh, yeah, sorry. The powers that be definitely want the knife so they can go over it carefully in a lab. Because Jasco is very clever, and smart, I can't do an easy drop. You know, carry a briefcase into a coffee shop, then pass it under the table to someone. Or leave a package on a park bench or whatever. Jasco has been around the block too many times for those types of deals."

"That makes sense."

"I still want him to come after me before he goes for you. I intend to force his hand, make him act when *I* decide. Hopefully he'll be a little careless."

Sophie nodded, not certain she could speak past the constricting lump in her throat.

"So, we're going to put on a real show. Tonight you and I are going to a megabucks charity ball at the Empire Hotel. During the evening, I'll pass the knife to the agent who will be there. I'm counting on Jasco to be there, too. If you, as a private citizen, are willing to go

with this, the suits will stand back and let you do it." He
shook his head. "Damn it, I don't like it."

Sophie leaned forward in her chair. "I *want* to be involved, Tyson. You know how I feel about this whole
thing. Yes, I get frightened at times, I admit that, but I
can't just hide in a corner until it's over." She smiled.
"I'm eager to see you in a tuxedo. You'll be absolutely
gorgeous."

Tyson glowered at her. "I hate wearing one of those
things. Lord, a grown man with ruffles on his shirt. Well,
they're tucks or pleats or whatever the hell you call them,
but they're still ridiculous."

Sophie laughed. "You're pouting. You're actually
pouting because you have to impersonate a penguin."

"Sophie," he said gruffly, getting to his feet, "don't
push it." He strode toward the kitchen.

Sophie stifled another burst of laughter.

Oh, my, she thought, she loved Tyson MacDonald
very, very much.

In the kitchen, Tyson poured himself another mug of
coffee, realized he didn't want it and set the mug in the
sink. He gripped the edge of the counter so tightly that
his knuckles turned white and a muscle jumped in his
clenched jaw.

He did *not,* he thought fiercely, want Sophie caught up
any further in this dangerous mess. He did *not* want Sophie in the same city, on the same planet, with Jasco. The
way things were set up, Tyson had no choice but to lead
Sophie by the hand right into the middle of the fray,
damn it. And he did *not* want to continue to lie to her
about Hank.

Whatever it took, he vowed, he'd keep Sophie safe, out of harm's way. Nothing, *nothing,* was going to happen to her because . . .

He drew a shaking hand down his face.

Because he loved her. He was in love with Sophie Clarkson.

The emotion churning within him that he'd refused to give name to was hammering at him from all sides, giving no quarter.

Love . . . love . . . love.

He had *made* love, and he was *in* love with Sophie. And he was terrified. To love was to dream of a future, a forever, with that special someone. He didn't know how to think of the future, had dreamed only the one scenario—the house, the grass to mow, Buddy the dog.

But now in his mind's eye, Tyson saw Sophie inside the house with Soapy the cat. Sophie holding in her arms the child that they, Sophie and Tyson together, had created in love. Sophie waiting to welcome him home . . . home . . . home.

"No," he said, the sound a harsh whisper.

It wasn't a dream, he thought; it was a *pipe dream*—out of his reach, beyond his grasp. Sophie would never love him because he was one of them, from the dark side of life. She wouldn't forgive him for being a part of the cruel lie about Hank. The deck was definitely stacked against him. Even if he quit the agency, Sophie would know who he had been, what he had done.

He was in love for the first time in his life, and the declaration of that love would never be put into words.

When Jasco had been caught or killed, when all of this was over and Sophie was no longer in danger, then Tyson would, he knew, walk out of her life forever.

He would spend the remainder of his days alone, and now, he realized, he would spend the remainder of his days lonely.

Eleven

———

Sophie Clarkson was the most beautiful woman he had ever seen.

That thought echoed in Tyson's mind over and over, causing heat to coil low in his body and his blood to pound, thunder, to the point of creating a rushing noise in his ears.

How long he had been staring at the exquisite creation who was Sophie, he had no idea, nor did he wish to end his scrutiny of her as he tucked every detail carefully into the Tyson's attic of his heart. When she had stepped into the living room, everything but Sophie had seemed to disappear.

This woman, he realized, this epitome of femininity, had touched his soul and captured his heart. She had warmed a place within him that he had not realized until now had been chilled. He loved her, although she would never know, for to declare that love would serve no purpose.

The dark and lonely days and nights that would stretch into infinity when he left her would be endured . . . somehow. Suddenly it seemed a small price to pay for the hours, minutes, seconds, he now shared with her.

Standing there before him, he mused, she was a vision of beauty, but he had no words within his reach to tell her how moved he was by the mere sight of her.

Her hair, he saw, was swept up into a soft halo of silken waves on the top of her head, with small curls escaping to caress her cheeks and trail along the satiny skin of her slender neck, which seemed to be beckoning to him to pay homage to with his lips.

Her dress was ice blue velvet, making her eyes appear even larger, and as richly blue and clear as a warm summer sky. The scalloped neckline was cut low, baring her shoulders and giving a hint of lush breasts, her skin like the finest alabaster. The material of the short-sleeved dress hugged her figure, nipping at the waist, sloping gently over her hips to stop just above knees that accentuated shapely calves.

She wore no jewelry, Tyson noted, and needed none, for Sophie glowed, sparkled, simply by being far, far brighter than any priceless gem that might be found anywhere in the world.

"Ah, Sophie," he said, his voice gritty with passion and emotion, "you're so damn beautiful."

Sophie smiled her thank-you for Tyson's heartfelt compliment, knowing her voice would fail her if she tried to speak. The sight of Tyson in the perfectly cut tuxedo had taken her breath away at the same moment desire's heat had created a flush on her cheeks.

So tall, she mused dreamily, so strong and masculine was this man she loved, her Tyson MacDonald. The fussy shirt with gold studs, the bow tie, the velvet lapels on the black jacket, did nothing to diminish the blatant aura of virility that emanated from him.

He was destined to break her heart, to leave her weeping in the night. But now, right now, he was hers. And, oh, how deeply she loved him.

"You're wonderfully handsome," she said, hearing the thread of breathlessness in her voice, "and you think I'm beautiful. Together, then, Tyson, we're . . . well, we must be sensational."

He smiled, a very male, very sensual, very enticing smile that caused Sophie's pulse to race.

"Oh, yes, Sophie Clarkson," he said, his voice flowing over her and through her like warm, rich brandy, "together we are *definitely* sensational."

Twelve

The spell of heated sexual awareness and tension that had seemed to virtually crackle through the air in the living room was shattered the moment that Sophie and Tyson stepped outside to be greeted by a clear, bitterly cold night.

"We'll take your car," Tyson said, still holding Sophie's key chain after locking the door. "Red is definitely easier to keep track of in heavy traffic. I want Jasco—assuming he's watching us—to have no problem following us to the hotel."

Sophie nodded.

"I made a giant production," Tyson went on, "of pretending to have difficulty earlier in locking my car door so he could get a good look at the tuxedo. He's had plenty of time to decide on a disguise and at least a tentative plan of action. We have to remember that he doesn't know if we're going to a small, private party, or to a big deal. All he has is the information that it's fancy. He'll have to adjust at the last minute.''

''Tyson, what if he doesn't do any of this?'' Sophie said. ''You know, maybe he'll feel it would be too crowded at the Empire or whatever.''

''Then I'll think of some other way to smoke him out. But my instincts say this will bring him to the surface. I'm counting on him being angry that the knife didn't get a lot of attention, and I've dealt with a few nut cases in my day, Sophie. I honestly believe that Jasco will make his move tonight.''

''Wonderful,'' she said dryly. ''I can hardly wait.''

''We don't have to go, Sophie.''

''No, no, I'm fine. Let's get in the car before my toes freeze.''

As they drove away from the house, the reality of where they were going, and why, demanded its due, causing them both to withdraw into their own private thoughts. Since Tyson had been given directions for finding the Empire Hotel, it wasn't necessary for Sophie to act as navigator.

A strained silence hung over the interior of the car like a dark, brewing storm cloud.

When they were within several miles of the hotel, Tyson attempted to lighten the somber mood. He tapped one fingertip against the battered ballerina charm on the key chain.

''Fair warning, Miss Twinkle Toes,'' he said. ''Just because you had dancing lessons as a kid doesn't mean that I did. My quota at functions like this is one dance— hear that?—*one.*''

Sophie looked over at him and smiled. ''I bet you're a very good dancer.''

"No, not even close. I'm a dud. You'll be all right, though. Broken toes don't take long to heal."

"How comforting," she said, laughing. Her smile faded as she looked at the tiny ballerina. "I didn't have dancing lessons, Tyson. I dug in my heels when I was eight or nine, and refused because dance lessons would take up the time I wanted to have to play baseball. My dad finally threw up his hands and admitted defeat. He even bought me a new baseball mitt."

"Poor Hank," Tyson said, chuckling.

"Well, he..." Sophie stopped speaking and stiffened, her gaze riveted on the gold charm. "Tyson—"

"What's wrong?" He glanced over at her, then quickly redirected his attention to the surging traffic.

"Do you remember when I didn't throw a fit when you said you were moving in with me?"

"Sure. You really got me going."

"Yes, by acting like Hank's daughter, by doing the exact opposite of what was expected, just the way he'd described to me many times over the years."

"And?" Tyson said, obviously confused.

"Don't you see?" she said, leaning towards him. "The charm on the key chain. You naturally assumed that it meant that I had dancing lessons as a little girl, but it was just the opposite. That charm, Tyson, is shouting a message, saying, 'Hey, this isn't what you think it is, so pay attention to what it *really* is.'"

"Oh, man, you're coming across loud and clear. Inside that charm is..."

"...the microdot," Sophie finished for him.

"You're something, Sophie Clarkson," he said quietly. "Hank would be bursting with pride."

"Well, we don't know if I'm right."

"We'll soon find out. We don't need gas, but I'm going to pull into the service station up ahead and have the attendant look under the hood. I'll tell him that I think a belt is slipping. While I'm doing that, and the car is off, pull out the key and take the charm off of the key chain."

"All right."

At the station, Tyson gestured to the interior of the car under the hood while a rather bemused young man slowly shook his head. Sophie quickly removed the charm from the key chain, then returned the proper key to the ignition.

Keeping her hand well out of view, she stared at the charm in her palm.

"Yes? No?" she whispered. "Have I understood what you were saying, Dad? Is the microdot inside this little dancer?"

She glanced up to be certain that Tyson and the attendant were still occupied, then opened her silver clutch purse and removed a fingernail file. With steady hands she slid the pointed end around the edge of the charm ... once, twice, then gasped as she found the minute hole. With a twist of the file, the charm popped open.

A small, cellophane-covered black dot was lying inside the charm.

"I heard you, Dad," she said, sudden tears misting her eyes. "You spoke to me, and I listened. Oh, dear Lord, I wish you were here."

Sophie jumped as the hood of the car was slammed shut. Tyson gave the attendant a folded bill, then got back into the vehicle.

"Anything?" he said, starting the ignition and driving forward.

"It's here, Tyson," Sophie said, her voice trembling. "I pried open the charm, and the microdot is inside."

Tyson reached over and squeezed one of her hands without looking at her.

"You did it, Sophie," he said.

"My father," she said, blinking away her tears, "my father successfully completed his last assignment. I hope he somehow knows that." She shook her head as her emotions choked off her words.

Ah, Sophie, Tyson's mind hammered, don't cry. God, he wanted to pull to the side of the road, take Sophie into his arms, tell her that Hank was alive, though barely.

It was so wrong, just so damn cruel, to continue this subterfuge. Maybe Hank would never regain consciousness, but Sophie had the right to at least see her father and say goodbye. But he had his orders. He had to keep silent . . . for now.

"Sophie," he said, "do you have a handkerchief to put the charm in?"

"Yes."

"Wrap it up and slip it into my jacket pocket. I'll pass it on with the knife to my contact at the hotel." He paused. "Are you up to this? I can do this differently if you want to go home."

"No, we'll stick to the plan," she said, lifting her chin. "There's the hotel just up ahead." She followed Tyson's instructions and placed the handkerchief containing the charm in his pocket. "You must be so cold from standing that long in the open at that service station without a heavy coat."

"Sheepskin jackets and tuxedos don't quite cut it on the fashion scene." He hesitated. "Sophie, are you positive that you want to—"

"Tyson," she interrupted, "the turn lane for the hotel is just up ahead there. Prince Charming, take me to the ball."

* * *

At the hotel, Tyson left the keys in the ignition for the uniformed valet, then came around to assist Sophie from the vehicle. She wore a fake-fur-lined coat that complemented her dress and carried the small silver clutch purse.

As they walked up the broad steps to the entrance of the elegant structure, Sophie slipped one arm through Tyson's.

"What does our contact look like, Clyde?" she suddenly said out of the corner of her mouth. She continued to gaze straight ahead, a pleasant expression on her face.

Tyson's head snapped around to stare at her, the motion nearly causing him to stumble.

"Clyde?" he repeated, then hooted with laughter. "Oh, Lord, you're incredible. But that, Bonnie, is something you don't need to know."

"You're no fun."

"Oh? That's not what you said last night."

"Tyson MacDonald," she said, shooting him a glare, "hush your mouth."

"Yes, ma'am," he said, then laughed again and shook his head.

Inside the hotel, Tyson produced the required engraved invitation, then Sophie's coat was checked. They were given instructions for locating the ballroom being used for the event.

The momentary lighthearted exchange they'd shared was replaced by tension, by the realization that dangerous events could very well unfold before the night was over.

They entered the huge ballroom to find that several hundred people had already arrived and a ten-piece band was playing. Small tables surrounded a gleaming, crowded dance floor, and a multitude of glittering chandeliers hung from the ceiling. The men were uniformly attired in dark tuxedos; the women's gowns created a rainbow of colors. A lavish buffet with an ice-sculptured swan in the center was against one wall.

"My goodness," Sophie said, "isn't this snazzy?"

"If you're into swans melting all over your food," Tyson said. "Come on, let's mingle. You're awfully pale, Sophie. Are you sure you're all right?"

"Tyson, I'm fine. Terrified, but fine. Give me a hint as to who we're meeting? Man? Woman? Old? Young?"

"Correction, *I'm* meeting with him."

"Him?" she said. "It's a man?"

Tyson planted a quick kiss on her lips. "Forget it, Bonnie."

"You're a mean man, Clyde."

For the next hour, Sophie and Tyson wandered around the edge of the room, each holding a champagne glass but not drinking from it. The throng of people, although strangers, were friendly and in a festive mood, inviting them to stop and chat.

The time passed with agonizing slowness, and Sophie was acutely aware that her nerves were becoming more frazzled by the moment.

Tyson, she realized, gave the appearance of a relaxed, confident man who was enjoying a lavish evening on the town. But she saw the quick darting of his eyes that encompassed the party goers, as well as the roaming waiters. She could feel the tight set of his muscles as she curled her fingers around his upper arm, and saw the occasional increased tempo of the pulse beating in his temple.

Tyson was on full alert, she knew, for any sign of Jasco. Was that horrible creature actually here, disguised beyond their recognition? Dear heaven, the waiting and watching was maddening.

And to increase her ever-growing tension was the knowledge that the microdot that had cost her beloved father his life was right there in Tyson's pocket, wrapped in a delicate Irish linen hankie edged with lace. Would this nightmare never end?

"It's time for my yearly dance," Tyson said finally. "I can get a closer look at some people while we're on the dance floor."

"All right. Oh, they're playing a lovely waltz."

Sophie moved eagerly into Tyson's embrace and instantly felt as though she were floating on a cloud. Despite Tyson's remarks to the contrary, he was an excellent dancer, gliding across the floor with the same easy grace with which he always moved. Sophie dreamily decided that the song should last a year and a day, but the final note was played. Tyson took her hand and led her from the floor, weaving through the tables to reach the wall.

"Did I step on your—" Tyson started, then stopped and narrowed his eyes as he looked beyond her. He met her gaze again. "Sophie, go powder your nose, okay?"

Sophie frowned. "I never powder my nose. What's wrong with my nose?" She blinked. "Oh! You want me to disappear so that you can find the agent you're meeting. Well, so be it, darn it. How long should I powder?"

"Ten minutes. I'll meet you back here."

She brushed her lips over his. "Ten minutes," she said. *I love you, Tyson MacDonald.* "I'll be waiting for you." *For the rest of my life.* "Bye." She waved at him, then began to weave her way through the people in her path to reach the door of the ballroom.

Tyson watched her go, acutely aware of a prickly sensation that was jumping along his spine and a tight knot in his gut.

Trouble, his inner voice nagged. *Something was wrong.* He was standing there seeing Sophie disappear from his view as she followed *his* orders, while familiar signals that had held him in good stead over the years were telling him that *something was wrong.*

"Damn," he said under his breath.

He tore his gaze from the direction Sophie had gone, then started across the crowded room. A few minutes later, he plastered a bright, phony smile on his face as he approached a plump, short woman in her seventies whose peach-colored evening gown was accompanied by a large peach shawl that encased her shoulders and fell to her knees.

"Mabel," he said, waving, "I thought that was you. I haven't seen you in years, not since you baby-sat me that time my parents went to Europe."

"Oh, my darling Tyson," the elderly woman said. "Isn't this a wonderful surprise?" She swept her gaze over the five people in the group she was chatting with. "This is like a Christmas present, seeing Tyson again." The people smiled and nodded. "You come give your Auntie Mabel a big hug. Oh, haven't you grown up to be the handsomest thing? Here I am, a tottering old spinster, and I feel as though I'm being united with my own little boy. Hug, hug, hug, Tyson. Let me get my hands on you."

Tyson managed a hollow-sounding laugh and moved into the woman's embrace, hearing murmured, "Oh, how lovely" and "It's enough to bring tears to my eyes," from two of the women watching.

The hug was executed, along with Mabel's smacking kiss on Tyson's cheek, then he stepped back.

"Mabel," he said, "now that I've found you again I'm going to take you to dinner at the fanciest restaurant in town. I'll call you. Are you in the book?"

"Oh, yes, darling, and I'll be looking forward to it. Goodbye for now."

Tyson smiled at her, nodded at the other people, then walked away.

The knife and the handkerchief containing the micro-dot and charm were now securely concealed beneath Auntie Mabel's flowing shawl.

Sophie followed the signs done in Old English script with an arrow beneath the word Ladies. As she turned the third corner in her journey, she stopped so quickly that she teetered on her shoes.

A foot-high, bright yellow plastic tripod sign sat in the middle of the corridor, announcing to anyone who read it that this was a Wet Floor. Beyond the barrier a man in a coverall was sloshing a string mop over the tile. A bucket on wheels half-full of murky water was close by.

"Oh," Sophie said. "Well, it's rather early to be cleaning up for the night, but could you tell me where another ladies' room is?"

The man continued his back-and-forth motion with the mop, not acknowledging Sophie's presence.

"Sir?" she said.

"No English," he said.

"I see. Well, thank you."

"No English."

"Right," she said, then turned and walked slowly away.

She could, she supposed, just wander on back to the
ballroom and use up the remaining minutes by strolling
along. Then again, she might as well visit the powder
room while the opportunity presented itself—providing,
of course, she could find one that didn't have a wet floor
blocking the entrance.

Nothing like a rest-room treasure hunt, she thought
dryly, to give one a short mental recess from the formidable subject of Jasco.

Tyson looked at his watch again, frowned, then attempted but failed to adopt a nonchalant expression.

Where was Sophie? he mentally asked for the umpteenth time. She was late returning to where they were to
meet. Yeah, so, okay, three minutes late wasn't a major
crime, but...

He scanned the crowd again, willing Jasco to suddenly appear.

Nice try, MacDonald, Tyson thought, but he'd still bet
his last dime that Jasco was in that hotel. Disguised as
what? Waiting for what before he made his move? Sophie was safe enough in the powder room, as it would be
filled with chattering women.

Maybe, Tyson pondered, Jasco would surface in the
parking lot. But then he realized that the valets would be
there, bringing the vehicles to the brightly lit front of the
building. He was going to have to lure Jasco into the open
with more inventive methods. Yes, he and Sophie would
wander off to the quiet, candlelit piano lounge near the
lobby, giving the impression they'd had enough of the
noise and hubbub of the ballroom.

Good. It was good. But where was Sophie?

Tyson's muscles twitched from tension, and he left the
huge room.

He'd meet Sophie on her way back from the powder room, he decided. He'd suggest they have a quiet drink in the lounge. Sophie was sharp. She'd pick up on the fact that Tyson had changed plans and was speaking carefully in case Jasco was somehow listening.

Tyson nodded in satisfaction and quickened his step. He would not, he knew, rid himself of the knot in his gut and his sense of pending danger until the woman he loved was once more close to his side.

Fools, Jasco thought gleefully. Such ignorant fools he was dealing with. Their stupidity was nearly enough to take the challenge out of the game.

He shoved the bucket, mop and plastic sign into a utility closet, then stripped off the coverall. He removed the fake beard and the wig, then ran sweaty hands over the black sweater he wore with black slacks.

Now, he thought, he was ready. He'd watched Sophie Clarkson as she'd gone in search of a different ladies' room. He knew which direction she'd chosen, and now, at long last, his moment of triumph had come.

He was in control.

Thirteen

Sophie hurried along the hallway, but as she turned yet another corner, she slowed her pace and frowned.

This part of the hotel was a twisting, turning series of corridors, she thought, like a maze. The farther she went, the more quiet it became, the only sounds being the tapping of her heels on the tile floor and the echo in her ears of her suddenly racing heart. The lighting was dimmer, too, casting an eerie glow over the hallways.

She stopped walking and glanced around, her grip on her clutch purse tightening. She felt a sudden chill and a sense of foreboding, as though she were being warned from a source unknown that she shouldn't be there, that... Yes, the sensation was strong now, she realized, the message clear: danger. *Danger!*

Tyson, she thought. She was going to be late meeting him, and he'd become concerned.

She took one step backward, another, then spun around with the intention of retracing her path and returning to the ballroom where, now, she just somehow knew, she belonged.

The piercing scream that started to escape from her throat was stifled by a hand being roughly clamped over her mouth.

Her eyes widened in horror as she stared at the man standing in front of her. In one terrifying instant, she cataloged every inch of him, like a camera producing a permanent picture in her mind.

He was short, no taller than she was herself, and he was thin, very thin. He had graying, greasy hair, small, narrowed eyes and a sneering smile. An ugly, purple, puckered scar ran jaggedly from his right eye down to the corner of his mouth, and in the hand that wasn't held tightly over her mouth was a knife.

Jasco!

A whimpering sob caught in Sophie's throat, replacing the smothered scream.

"We meet at last," Jasco said, his voice high-pitched. "You're pretty, I'll give you that, Sophie Clarkson, but you won't be for long." He moved the knife closer to her face. Sophie shivered. "I'm going to take my hand away, but if you make one sound, I'll cut you. Understand?"

Sophie nodded as she blinked away sudden tears, refusing to allow them to spill onto her cheeks. Jasco slowly withdrew his hand. He gripped her upper arm so tightly she winced.

"We're getting out of here," Jasco said, "before your boyfriend comes looking for you. You dumped the lawyer for a government agent, huh? Oh, yes, I know MacDonald. I'm going to get him, too, just because

Hank liked him so much. Yeah, yeah, that's a nice touch. I'll kill you *and* MacDonald.''

''No,'' Sophie said, ''please, no. You're making a terrible mistake. Tyson has nothing to do with you. He's on vacation, and he's leaving soon.''

''Oh, my,'' Jasco said, his voice dripping with sarcasm, ''aren't you the loyal little romantic?'' A sneer curled his lips. ''You can't protect MacDonald from me. No one is safe from me once I decide they're to die. And you *and* your lover are very definitely going to die. I saw to it that Hank Clarkson was killed. I won't be stopped until I've finished what I set out to do.''

The chilling cold of fear that was coursing through Sophie was swept away by a sudden rush of hot fury, causing a flush on her pale cheeks.

''You're an animal,'' she said, her voice quivering with rage. ''You killed my father for revenge, but that won't change the fact that you'll go to your grave with my father's mark on you.''

''Shut up,'' Jasco yelled. The hand holding the knife shook, and a wild cast glinted in his eyes. ''Shut your mouth, you evil woman. I'm in control of everything. You'll give me the microdot.''

Tyson flattened himself against the wall, his jaw clenched so tightly that his teeth ached as he listened to Sophie and Jasco.

Tyson had gone in the direction the arrows on the signs had indicated and had found the wet section of floor. He'd mentally pieced together the evidence he had as he stared at the glistening tile, then had spun on his heel and strode down the corridor in the opposite direction.

And now, thank God, he thought, he'd found Sophie. He was only moments too late, precious moments that could cost Sophie her life if he made the slightest error.

A trickle of sweat ran down Tyson's back. He unbuttoned his tuxedo jacket and reached to the back of his belt for his gun.

Easy, Sophie, he mentally directed. Don't push Jasco too far. Keep him occupied, but don't make him totally lose it. Easy, my love, easy.

Tyson moved away from the wall and stepped around the corner. Jasco and Sophie were approximately four feet in front of him, with Jasco's back to Tyson.

Sophie glanced up and saw Tyson and the shake of his head telling her not to react to his arrival. She quickly looked at Jasco again as her heart beat with a painful tempo.

"No, I won't shut up, you creep," she said to Jasco. "Why should I? You're going to kill me, so why should I take orders from you? Or maybe you're not brave enough to kill me. You're a phony, taking credit for my father's death when all of us know you hired someone else to do it. You're a coward, and there's no reason for me to think otherwise."

Tyson inched his way forward.

"Yes, I know how it really was," Sophie went on. "You didn't kill Hank. Your hired help had to do it for you."

"Shut up. Shut up. Yes, I did," Jasco hollered, waving the knife in front of Sophie's face. "I was there. I gave the orders. I was in control, just like I am now. I want the microdot, and you'll give it to me."

Jasco threw back his head and laughed, an unearthly sound causing a shiver to shimmer through Sophie.

Tyson closed the remaining distance separating him from Jasco, and at that exact moment, Sophie thrust out her hands and shoved against Jasco's chest. He staggered, then Tyson flung one arm around Jasco's neck.

With strength born of insanity, Jasco rammed his elbow into Tyson's stomach, causing Tyson's grip to loosen just enough to allow the captured man to break free and swing the knife, the gleaming blade slicing through the material of Tyson's jacket as easily as cutting softened butter.

"Damn," Tyson said as hot pain radiated through his upper chest and across his shoulder, causing him to drop his gun. The weapon slid across the polished floor to rest against the wall. "Damn you, Jasco."

"You're dead, you're dead," Jasco said in a singsong voice.

"Forget it," Tyson said, feeling the warm blood soaking through his clothes and running down his arm. "I have backups, Jasco. Every exit is covered by my men." Not true, but if Jasco believed it . . . "You're finished."

"No one can help you," Jasco said. "No one, because I'm in control. You're a fool, MacDonald. Everyone is under my power."

"Except me," Sophie said, the gun held in both hands and pointed at Jasco. "Look what I found just sitting on the floor. Drop the knife, Jasco, or I swear to heaven I'm going to pull this trigger.

"No-o-o," Jasco screamed. "You can't kill me. I've got to do what I came here for. I need the microdot. I need to kill both of you. You can't stop me now."

"Drop that knife," Sophie repeated.

"No!" Jasco started toward her.

As Jasco shifted, Tyson lowered his uninjured shoulder and slammed into Jasco's body, sending the smaller man crashing to the floor. The knife flew from Jasco's hand and skittered several feet away along the floor. Jasco hit his head against the wall.

Tyson regained his balance, a wave of dizziness assaulting him as he clamped his hand over his burning shoulder, seeing the drops of blood dripping onto the floor from the tips of his fingers.

Jasco curled into a fetal position on the floor and rocked back and forth, a sobbing moan accompanying the motion while he held his head.

"Tyson?" Sophie whispered. "Tyson?"

"It's over," he said, his voice strained as he fought the pain rocketing through his body. "Put the gun on the floor, Sophie. Carefully."

"Yes." Sophie set the gun on the floor. "Tyson, you're hurt, you're..."

"Call the police. Hurry. Go on."

"But you're bleeding!"

"Do it, Sophie," he said, leaning against the wall. "We'll let the agency answer the cops' questions. Go, before I pass out. You were wonderful, terrific. Hank will be, would have been proud of you. Go. It's over, Sophie. It's all over. Everything."

"I'll call," she said. "I'll hurry." She took off at a run.

During the following hours, Sophie did as she was instructed by the police, then men in suits and ties and later the doctor at the hospital where Tyson's wound was treated. She'd been subdued and cooperative, agreeing to be driven home without having been allowed to see Tyson even for a moment.

The doctor had assured her that, while Tyson's wound was deep and very painful, he would be fine if he didn't try to rush the recovery process. Tyson was sleeping with the aid of a massive shot of painkiller, and Sophie could visit him the next day.

She had thanked the doctor, smiled politely at the various men surrounding her and left the hospital with her escort. The man told her there was something of extreme importance to discuss with her, but urged her to get a solid night's sleep first. Men from the agency would be in touch with her the next day. Sophie nodded absently.

But through it all she heard Tyson's words echoing over and over in her head, taunting her, causing a cold fist to seem to clutch her heart.

It's over, Sophie. It's all over. Everything.

Fourteen

Tyson slowly surfaced from a deep, drug-induced sleep and opened his eyes to find the hospital room flooded with bright sunlight. He shifted slightly on the bed, then instantly regretted the motion as grinding pain shot through his shoulder, chest and arm.

"Good morning," a man's voice said, "Special Agent MacDonald."

Tyson turned his head on the pillow, then frowned. "Leonard, you're the last person on earth I'd choose to wake up to see."

The impeccably dressed man in his early fifties chuckled. He sat in a chair next to the bed, his elbows propped on the wooden arms, his fingertips touching to form a steeple.

"One of these days," Leonard said, smiling, "I'm going to write you up for being disrespectful to your superior officer, your boss, or whatever the hell I am."

"Go for it," Tyson said, "but you'd better make it quick, because the first chance I get *I'm* going to be writing my letter of resignation."

Leonard's smile faded, and he sighed. "I can't say I'm surprised because I've seen it coming for a while. I assume I'd be wasting my breath if I attempted to change your stubborn mind?"

"Guaranteed. I'm finished with the agency, Len. I've had enough."

Leonard nodded. "I know. I'll miss you, Mac-Donald. You and Hank were rebels, mavericks, but you were my two top men. He told me before he went on that last assignment that he was calling it quits when he got back."

"How's Sophie?" Tyson asked, "and what's the latest word on Hank?" He winced as fiery pain rocketed through him again.

"You're supposed to be resting," Len said. "I just wanted to make certain that you were all right. Jasco, by the way, is under wraps, and we've passed the microdot on to the proper people. You did a very nice job, and Sophie Clarkson was no slouch, either, according to the report I got. You two were quite a team. Of course, so were you and Hank."

"Would you cut the chitchat?" Tyson said. "The last thing I remember about last night is a bunch of uniforms and suits swarming over the place, then the floor came up to meet me. Damn it, Len, is Sophie all right?"

Leonard raised both hands in a gesture of peace. "Yes, yes, she's fine. She gave us a full report, then one of our guys took her home. I think she was a little dazed by what had happened, but a good night's sleep will have remedied that. Two of our men are on the way over there right now to tell her about Hank being alive."

Tyson's eyes narrowed, and his voice was ominously quiet and low when he spoke. "What? What did you say?"

"Well, she deserves to be told the truth, so I sent agents this morning before she left there to come visit you. I do believe the lady is smitten with you, chum. Oh, she didn't say anything, but I still have my gut instincts. Anyway, we'll fly her to Washington, D.C. this afternoon to see Hank. I imagine she'll come here first, though."

"You louse," Tyson said, attempting to rise. Pain immediately stopped him, and he sank back against the pillow with a groan. Cold sweat beaded his brow as he clutched his shoulder, which was covered in heavy layers of white gauze, as was half of his chest. "You've got as much sensitivity as a rock," he said, his voice strained.

Leonard got to his feet and walked to the foot of the bed. "Don't start on me, MacDonald. You know it was the best security plan to keep things status quo. Hank's safety was a major concern. It all worked out for the best in the end."

"Oh, yeah, right. Two strangers are going to waltz into Sophie's house and say, 'Oh, by the way, your father is still alive. We were stringing you for a while there, lady.' Damn it, Len, *I* should have been the one to tell her."

Leonard stared at Tyson for a long moment, then slowly nodded. "So that's the way the wind blows. I didn't think there was a woman born who could snag you, MacDonald." He chuckled. "Hank Clarkson's daughter. Now isn't that something? Hank will be extremely pleased about this, I'm sure."

"Len," Tyson said, through clenched teeth, "you get on the phone, call those two yo-yos on their beepers and tell them *not* to go to Sophie's."

"It's too late to catch them, Tyson. Look, she'll understand once it's laid out for her. She'll be so thrilled that Hank is alive that she won't care that you didn't tell her straight off."

"The hell she won't," Tyson said wearily, then closed his eyes.

"Well, Hank will talk turkey to her. Don't worry about it."

"Hank may never come out of that coma," Tyson said, his eyes still closed.

"Oh...that." Len ran one hand over the back of his neck. "Actually, Tyson, Hank surfaced two days ago."

Tyson's eyes flew open. "He...I've called in every day to check on... Why in the hell did you give orders to lie to me?"

"Just covering all the bases. Good thing I did, too. I decided that if you were at all attracted to Sophie and knew that Hank was awake, you just might tell her the truth. But attracted? Not even close. I can see you're down for the count...big-time."

"Len, I'm coming up out of this bed, and I'm going to deck you," Tyson said, fury ringing in his voice.

"Would you relax? They'll smack a No Visitors sign on your door if you don't calm down." He shook his head. "You're a helluva agent, but you don't know squat about the workings of women's minds."

"Sophie will..."

"Sophie," Leonard said, his voice rising, "will understand why you lied to her about her father being alive, MacDonald."

Sophie stood outside the closed door that showed the number the nurse at the station had given her. Instructions had been left, the nurse said, stating that Sophie

Clarkson was to be allowed to see Tyson MacDonald at any time and should not be required to wait for the designated visiting hours.

Sophie's right hand was raised in a loose fist to knock on the door, but she didn't move or hardly breathe. A chill swept through her, accompanied by a momentary wave of dizziness.

Just as she had reached the proper door, she'd heard a man, whose voice she didn't recognize, speak an unbelievable sentence. The words echoed unmercifully in her mind: *Sophie will understand why you lied to her about her father being alive, MacDonald.*

Without being totally aware that she was moving, Sophie pushed open the door and entered the room on trembling legs.

"Sophie!" Tyson said as she came into view. "Len, put the bed up."

"I don't know if you're allowed to be—" Leonard started.

"Do it," Tyson said.

Leonard sighed and pressed a button on the foot of the bed, raising Tyson to a semisitting position.

"Miss Clarkson," Leonard said, smiling at her.

She stood just inside the now-closed door, her gaze riveted on Tyson, no readable expression on her pale face.

"I assume," Len went on, "that my men have been to see you, have given you the good news about Hank."

"No," Sophie said, her voice shaking as she continued to stare at Tyson, "I haven't spoken with anyone this morning. I was so worried about Tyson that I decided to come over here. I heard a few words as I came to the door. My father is alive? He *didn't* die? You've known it all along, Tyson MacDonald, and I'm supposed to understand why you lied to me?''

"Sophie . . ." Tyson said.

"Now, Miss Clarkson," Len said, "Tyson can explain everything. This was done for Hank's safety, you see. He was in a deep coma, we didn't even know if he was going to make it, but he'll be fine. He's been awake for a couple of days and he's eager to see you."

Sophie's head snapped around, and her eyes were flashing with anger as she looked at Leonard.

"And if he hadn't come out of the coma?" she said. "What then? If he'd died without regaining consciousness, would you have said, 'Oh, well, that's the breaks,' and never told me that my father really wasn't in the casket you sent home?"

"That's a moot point, isn't it?" Len said. "It's not important now. Hank *is* alive."

"Get out, Len," Tyson said. "Go. *Now.*"

"Right. I'll check with you later." Leonard quickly left the room.

Sophie redirected her attention to Tyson and moved to stand next to him.

"You are," she said, her voice quivering, "the most despicable man I have ever known."

"Sophie, give me a chance to—"

"To what? Use up the rest of your arsenal of lies? Dear God, Tyson, how can you justify what you did? I was in pain, mourning the death of my father. I cried in your arms, wept because my heart was breaking. You could have spared me all that agony but, oh, no, not super-agent MacDonald. You followed your orders to the letter. Don't you think going to bed with me was a bit beyond the call of duty?"

"Sophie, don't," he said, reaching out one hand toward her. She stepped backward, out of his reach. His arm fell heavily onto the bed. "I hated the deception, Sophie, but Jasco has uncanny instincts. He could have sensed, seen, a change in your attitude if I told you Hank was alive, in a coma but alive. It was too risky. It ripped me up to know how sad you were, but I had to play it out that way."

Sophie wrapped her hands around her elbows in a protective gesture. Tears filled her eyes, but she blinked them angrily away.

"Of course you did," she said, a bitter edge to her voice. "It's the agency first, the assignment. Everything else takes second seat. Once Hank regained consciousness, you could have arranged for me to at least speak with him on the phone, hear his voice. You knew by then that I could do my part, perform properly, that I was capable of handling what was going on. You wouldn't even do that. You wouldn't even trust me enough for that."

"No, Sophie, that's not true. I didn't know that Hank..."

"Do you know why I came rushing over here this morning?" she said as though he hadn't spoken. "I was so worried about you, about what Jasco had done to you. And I was going crazy hearing your words beat against my brain."

"Words? What words?"

"Last night you said, 'It's over, Sophie. It's all over. Everything.' I had to know what that meant. Were you simply talking about the assignment, about Jasco, the microdot? Or did 'everything' include us, all that we'd shared?"

Unnoticed tears spilled onto her cheeks.

"I had to know," she went on, "because I'd fallen in love with you." She shook her head. "Silly me, huh? I was going to tell you that I'd accept the fact that you're an agent, would be there when you came home from assignments and...God, what a joke."

"Sophie, listen to me. I'm quitting the agency. I told Leonard that this morning."

"Oh, really? My, my isn't that nice? Now you can get your dog, Buddy. But that was probably just part of your act, too, right? The charming little hearth-and-home tale to give evidence as to how human you are, how real."

"Sophie, damn it, give me a chance to explain!"

"No! No, I don't want to hear any more of your lies. You're *not* human. You're a robot programmed by the agency." The tears continued to flow, running down her neck. "How did you keep from laughing, Tyson, when I told you about the Sophie's attic in my heart? It must have sounded so corny, so childish to you, the big macho agent."

"No. Ah, Sophie, no, I..."

"I'm leaving now, Tyson," she said, wiping the tears from her cheeks. "I'm going to my father. I'm going to a man who truly loves me, who has never lied to me, who I thought was dead but is gloriously alive. That's where *I'm* going. And you? You can go straight to hell." She turned and ran from the room.

"I'm already there," Tyson said to no one, his voice gritty. "Oh, God, Sophie, I love you so damn much."

Fifteen

Sophie set the tray holding a plate of sandwiches, two cups of coffee and a small bowl of fresh fruit on the low table between the sofa and the fireplace. She turned her head to frown at the leaping orange flames crackling in the hearth.

"Dad," she said, redirecting her attention to the man sitting on the sofa, "you started the fire again. You shouldn't be lifting those logs."

Hank Clarkson met Sophie's frown with one of his own. The resemblance between father and daughter would leave no doubt in a stranger's mind that the pair were related.

Hank was tall and trim, his thick, dark auburn hair peppered with gray. His eyes were the same shade of summer-sky blue as Sophie's. Hank's features were rough-hewn and craggy, would give a scrutinizing appraiser the delightful impression that a sculptor had stepped in to supervise the final touches of Sophie's, making hers smooth, soft, delicate and totally feminine.

"Sophie Clarkson," Hank said, "if you don't quit fussing over me like a mother hen, I'm going to ship myself back to that hospital in Washington."

"Eat your lunch," Sophie said, pointing to the tray. She came around the table to sit down next to him. "Pick up a sandwich and take a bite."

"I'm perfectly capable of coming to the table in the kitchen," Hank said. "In fact, I'm perfectly capable of fixing my own lunch. I'm also perfectly capable of turning you over my knee, darling daughter, and swatting your bottom if you don't stop fluttering around."

"Finished with your tantrum?" Sophie said, raising her eyebrows. "If so, commence with eating the sandwich that you see before you."

"That's it. That's all." Hank got to his feet and moved to the opposite side of the table. He crossed his arms over his chest and looked sternly at Sophie where she sat directly in front of him. "It's serious-talk time, young lady."

"Can't you eat and talk at the same time, Daddy dear?" she said ever so sweetly. "Now, come sit back down here and . . ."

"Soapy . . . stop!" Hank said, slicing one hand through the air.

Sophie opened her mouth to retort, decided it wasn't a terrific idea, considering the set to her father's jaw, and snapped her mouth closed. She settled for folding her arms beneath her breasts, sinking back on the sofa and issuing a nicely executed, indignant "Well!"

"Now, then," Hank said, lifting his chin in the exact same manner that Sophie was known to do, "are you going to listen?"

Sophie pursed her lips and nodded.

"Thank you. Sophie, I do *not* need a mother hen, a nursemaid or a baby-sitter. Yes, I was seriously wounded, but because of my superb physical condition..."

Sophie coughed.

Hank glared. "...superb physical condition, I'm recuperating with remarkable speed. It's been nearly a month since I came out of that coma. For two weeks of that I was in the Washington hospital being fussed at and being told to eat slimy Jell-O by a squadron of sadistic nurses. During the past two weeks since I've been home, you've taken up where those clucking chickens in white left off. You're at my house more than you're at your own home. You've practically turned Sophie's Attic over to Janet to run. You are, in short, driving me totally nuts."

"But Dad..."

"No," he said, shaking his head. "There will be no 'But Dad' during this dissertation. Sophie, I don't doubt for a minute that your concern for my well-being is sincere. On a conscious level, you're performing as any loving daughter would. However, I've drawn the conclusion that your subconscious is coming into play here, as well."

"My subconscious?"

Hank walked around the table and sat down again next to Sophie. His tone was gentle when he spoke.

"Honey," he said, "I've kept my mouth shut since I've been home with the hope that you'd come to your senses, but you apparently aren't going to do that. You've got that streak of Clarkson stubbornness in you, and this time it's not your best friend."

"What on earth are you talking about?"

Hank looked directly at her, blue eyes meeting blue eyes.

"Tyson MacDonald," he said quietly.

Sophie stiffened, and a warm flush stained her cheeks.

"I don't wish to discuss him," she said, wishing her voice was steadier.

"Tough. He's the topic now before the board. You and I are the board, by the way. Sophie, Tyson came to see me in the hospital in Washington."

Sophie's eyes widened. "You didn't tell me that." She paused. "Well, why should you? I mean, it's perfectly reasonable that he'd visit you. You've been close for many years."

"True," Hank said, nodding. "We compared our wounds and woes that were compliments of Jasco, and congratulated each other on having turned in our letters of resignation to the agency."

"Tyson really retired?"

"Yes, he did. Then Tyson and I talked, Sophie—friend to friend, man to man, father to son. Tyson opened up and spoke of his emotions, feelings, like I've never heard him do before. The subject was you."

"Oh," she said, aware of the increased tempo of her heart.

"Sophie, you know that Tyson did the right thing by following orders not to tell you that I was alive. In your heart of hearts, you realize that he really had no other choice."

"Yes, he did. Okay, I understand his silence at the beginning. But later? After what Tyson and I had . . . what we'd . . ."

"Try 'shared,'" Hank prompted.

The flush on Sophie's cheeks deepened to crimson.

"Yes, well, fine," she said, "what we shared. For Tyson to not, at that point, believe and trust in me enough to allow me to even speak to you on the phone is unforgivable. I felt betrayed, Dad, as though I'd been nothing more than a pawn to him, to be used as he saw fit in order to complete his assignment. I still feel that way. I also question everything he said and did."

"I see. Well, Sophie, there's a piece of information that you don't have. You're basing your attitude on the fact that Tyson should have bent, even broken, the rules of his orders and let you speak with me on the phone after I came out of the coma. You feel that your relationship had grown, deepened, to the extent that he should have been willing to do that."

"Yes," she said. "Yes, if he really cared about me—which he obviously doesn't—he wouldn't have stood silently by while I continued to mourn your death. You can lecture me from here to Sunday, and I won't change my mind. I could have heard your voice on the phone, could have put aside my grief. To deny me that was cruel on Tyson's part." She paused. "So what is this piece of information I don't have?"

"Are you certain that you want to know? You'll be forced to take a long look into the Sophie's attic in your heart to determine what to do once I tell you this."

"Yes, I want to know."

"All right. Sophie, Tyson was *not* aware that I had come out of the coma."

She stared at her father. "What?" she whispered.

"He was flat-out lied to because Len felt there was a risk that Tyson would do exactly what you've decided he should have. Tyson called in every day and was told there was no change in my condition. *Sophie, he didn't know.*"

Sophie pressed her fingertips to her lips as sudden tears misted her eyes.

"Oh, dear heaven," she said, her voice trembling, "what have I done?"

"You made a mistake. The important question is, what are you going to do about it? Sophie, honey, are you in love with Tyson MacDonald?"

She nodded as two tears slid down her cheeks. "Oh, yes, I love him so very much, Daddy. But I was so hurt that day in the hospital that I said some terrible things to him. Oh, good Lord, I even told him to go straight to hell."

Hank chuckled. "So he said." His smiled faded. "I urged Tyson to see you one more time, insist that you listen to him, hear the truth, but..." He shook his head. "He'd withdrawn, pulled back within himself."

"I know what you mean. He has walls that he stays behind to protect himself emotionally. He was lowering those walls...for me, telling me personal details and..." She sat straight upward. "Buddy. He even told me about Buddy."

"Who?"

"Dad, where is Tyson?"

"He went to Los Angeles to recuperate from Jasco's handiwork. But since Tyson is in superb physical condition—like your old man—he was up and at it in a flash."

"Dad, please, where is he?"

Hank smiled at her warmly. "Here. In Chicago. He's preparing to start a business that offers security systems, bodyguards, some supersleuthing, whatever. It will take time to determine what services draw the most clients. I just happen to have—" he reached into his shirt pocket and took out a folded piece of paper "—the address of the building he's renting an office in."

Sophie's hand was shaking as she took the paper.

"He's there now," Hank said. "He's painting the place because the landlord said if Tyson didn't like pea-soup-colored walls he could paint them at his own expense. Tyson doesn't like pea-soup-colored walls."

"I don't know what to say to him."

"You'll know when the time comes, when you're looking right at him. Will you just go and leave me in peace? Oh, sweet bliss, an entire afternoon with no mother hen."

Sophie leaned forward to kiss Hank on the cheek.

"Thank you, Dad. I love you."

"I love you, too, my girl. By happy, Soapy. That's all I've ever wanted for you."

She smiled, nodded, then got to her feet and hurried from the room.

With a very smug, very wise fatherly expression on his face, Hank reached for the plate of sandwiches.

Two hours later, Sophie stood in a corridor on the fourteenth floor of an office building on LaSalle Street, staring at a closed, solid-wood door.

She was nervous. She knew it, and none of the stern lectures she'd given herself on the way there about getting a grip on herself had helped one iota.

She swallowed heavily, lifted her chin, tightened her grip on the covered wicker basket she held in one hand, then opened the door and entered.

And there, his hair tousled, his ruggedly handsome face in need of a shave, his faded jeans and a sweatshirt with the sleeves raggedly cut off at the elbows splattered with paint, was Tyson MacDonald.

He was the most beautiful man she had ever seen.

Tyson stood statue still as their eyes met across the room. He was oblivious to the paint dripping from the roller onto the tennis shoes he wore.

Sophie, his mind thundered. *Sophie, I love you.*

Tyson, Sophie's heart sang. *My love, my life, my Tyson.*

"Hello, Tyson," she said, her voice unsteady.

"Sophie," he said, nodding slightly. There was no readable expression on his face, no warmth in his voice. "I'm surprised to see you here."

"Yes, well, I, Tyson, you're dripping paint on your shoes."

Tyson jerked, causing more white splatters to decorate the sweatshirt. He placed the roller in the pan, then straightened again, looking directly at her.

"How are you?" Sophie said. "I mean, how's your shoulder—where you were hurt?"

"Fine. I get a few twinges now and then, but that's to be expected. And you?"

"Oh, busy as a bee," she said, striving for a lightness to her voice that didn't quite materialize. She set the wicker basket on the floor.

"Going on a picnic?" Tyson said, glancing at the basket.

"No." She drew a deep breath, then let it out slowly, trying to calm her ever-increasing nervous state. "Tyson, we've covered the 'Hello, how are you?' formalities. I realize that you're in the middle of a project here, but I wondered if we could talk."

Tyson walked slowly forward, then stopped in the center of the room. He shoved his hands into his back pockets.

"What did you want to talk about, Sophie?"

So cold, Sophie thought. Tyson was, indeed, firmly behind his protective wall. Well, she was just going to have to tear them down, brick by brick if necessary.

"I came here," she said, "to apologize to you for my behavior that day at the hospital. Yes, I was stunned to learn that my father was alive, but that's no excuse for hurling accusations at you without giving you a chance to respond."

Sophie paused to allow Tyson to speak, but he said nothing.

"I, I meant what I said that day. I do love you, Tyson. I've missed you terribly and ... I was prepared to accept your life-style as an agent, but this new endeavor of yours sounds challenging and exciting. Oh, Tyson, I'm sorry I lashed out at you that day. I felt so betrayed, and then doubted everything concerning you. My father told me today that you didn't know that he'd come out of the coma, that the agency orders were to tell you that Hank's condition hadn't changed. If I would have given you a chance to speak, I wouldn't have spent such a miserable month."

Tyson still didn't respond.

"Or maybe I would have," Sophie said, feeling her patience slipping. "Maybe when you said that everything was over, you meant us, too. Damn it, Tyson MacDonald, would you say something? I feel like an idiot who's carrying on a one-sided conversation with a statue carved out of cold marble."

Again she waited, but there was only silence beating against her.

"Fine," she said, fighting against threatening tears. "I get the message. There's obviously more than one way to tell someone to go straight to hell. I screamed it in your face, you're saying it with icy silence. I'll leave you alone,

I'm going, but I just want you to know that what we had, those memories, will always have a special—" a sob caught in her throat "—place in Sophie's attic in my heart. Goodbye, Tyson MacDonald."

She turned and started toward the door, her vision blurred by tears that now spilled onto her cheeks.

"Sophie."

She stopped with her back to him, quickly swiping at the tears. Tyson's voice, she realized, sounded thick, strange, as though he was having difficulty speaking. She turned slowly to look at him, jumping slightly as she found him only several feet away. His hands were still in his back pockets, and his head was bent as though to scrutinize his paint-splattered shoes.

"Yes, Tyson?" she said tentatively.

"I, oh, God, I . . ."

He lifted his head to meet her gaze, and Sophie's breath caught as she saw the evidence of why Tyson hadn't spoken, hadn't responded. Her heart nearly burst with love as she realized what it was costing him to step from behind his barricade and reveal himself in such a vulnerable state.

He was trusting her with the very essence of himself.

Tyson MacDonald was crying.

He held out one shaking hand toward her. "I love you, Sophie," he said, emotions nearly choking his words. "I can't go on like this, missing you, wanting you, needing you. Needing you, Sophie, because you're the warm sunshine that can drive away the dark chill in my soul. Sophie, please, don't make me go through the rest of my life alone, because without you the alone has become lonely. Marry me, please. Be my wife, have my baby, put up with Buddy the dog, Soapy the cat and me. Please?"

Sophie hurled herself into Tyson's arms as fresh tears flowed down her cheeks. He encircled her with his arms, holding fast, burying his face in the fragrant cloud of her hair.

"Oh, Tyson, my answer is yes, yes, yes," she said, the tears still streaming down her face. "I love you, Tyson. I'll marry you, have your baby, adore your dog and cat and..."

Tyson lowered his head and captured her mouth in a searing kiss. It was a kiss of commitment, of love, of forever. It was a kiss of sunshine that caused warmth to course through them, then build into the welcomed heat of desire. It was a kiss that held the power to crush the final brick in Tyson's protective wall into dust.

"Let's get out of here," he said, close to her lips. "I want to make love with you for hours."

"What about the paint?"

"I'll hire someone to do it. I was getting more on me than on the walls. I'll—Sophie, whatever you have in that picnic hamper broke, because there's a wet puddle spreading beneath it."

"Oh, my gosh, I forgot. It didn't break...it emptied...sort of."

"What the—" Tyson started, then watched in wonder as one side of the hinged top rose and a small, furry head emerged.

"Tyson MacDonald," Sophie said with a sweep of her arm, "meet Buddy MacDonald."

"Aw, right," Tyson said with a whoop of laughter.

He gave Sophie another hard, toe-curling kiss, then lifted the puppy out of the basket. Buddy gave Tyson a sloppy kiss on the nose with a pale pink tongue.

"I like you, too," Tyson said to the dog. "I waited a long time for you, Buddy." He looked at Sophie. "And I waited a lifetime for you. Ah, Sophie, I love you."

"I love you, too, Tyson."

"Listen, I'm staying in a hotel for now. I don't think they'll allow Buddy in."

"Then let's go to Sophie's Attic," she said, slipping her arm through one of his.

"Okay. I want you to know that this day will always have a special place in the Tyson's attic in my heart."

Sophie smiled up at him, love shining in her eyes. Then Sophie, Tyson and Buddy, who was busily chewing a hole in the front of Tyson's sweatshirt, went home.

Epilogue

"Oh, Tyson," Sophie said, "this beach, the sun, is heavenly. A honeymoon in Hawaii. Perfect."

Tyson lay next to her on a towel, his eyes closed. "You won't think so if you get sunburned."

"True. Won't it be fun when we get back to see what Janet's brothers have finished of the projects on the house? Oh, Tyson, my father is so pleased to know his grandchildren are going to be raised in the house I grew up in."

"It's a great house. The addition for Hank's apartment will blend right in. I'm glad he agreed to work part-time at MacDonald Security. I'll really benefit from his expertise. Yeah, everything is so good."

"The first day home we must go to the pound to find Soapy the cat."

Tyson chuckled. "Okay."

"I love you, Mr. MacDonald."

"I love you, too, Mrs. MacDonald. I'll even love you when you look like a lobster."

"Oh, all right, I'll put on some more sunscreen." She sat up, then stiffened. "Tyson?" she whispered.

"Hmm? I think I'm asleep."

"No, you're not. Listen to me. It's her."

"Her who?" he said, not opening his eyes.

"Zula."

"Huh?"

"You know, that beautiful woman who wore the caftans and was connected to the counterfeiting ring."

"Oh, *that* Zula."

"Tyson, for pete's sake, open your eyes. She's walking down the beach."

"I seriously doubt that. Besides, I retired from that line of work, remember?"

"That does not, sir, excuse you from being a conscientious citizen. It stands to reason that Zula might very well be involved with another crook. It certainly should be checked out." She got to her feet. "I'm going to follow her." She took off at a run.

Tyson rolled to his feet and planted his hands on his hips. Smiling and shaking his head, he started after Sophie at a more leisurely pace.

Sophie was Hank's kid, all right, Tyson thought. A real chip off the old block. With his luck, that probably really *was* Zula. But Sophie had nothing to worry about because Tyson MacDonald was going to take care of her, and love her, until the day he died.

Tyson quickened his step, then started to sprint across the warm sand.

He was on his way to Sophie, and there was nowhere else on earth he wished to be.

*　　*　　*　　*　　*

THE DONOVAN LEGACY
from Nora Roberts

Meet the Donovans—Morgana, Sebastian and
Anastasia. They're an unusual threesome. Triple
your fun with double cousins, the only children of
triplet sisters and triplet brothers. Each one is
unique. Each one is. . . special.

In January you will be *Captivated* by Morgana
Donovan. In Special Edition 768, horror-film
writer Nash Kirkland doesn't know what to do
when he meets an actual witch!

Be *Entranced* in February by Sebastian Donovan in
Special Editon 774. Private investigator Mary
Ellen Sutherland doesn't believe in psychic
phenomena. But she discovers Sebastian has
strange powers. . . over her.

In March's Special Edition 780, you'll be *Charmed*
by Anastasia Donovan, along with Boone Sawyer
and his little girl. Anastasia was a healer, but for
her it was Boone's touch that cast a spell.

Enjoy the magic of Nora Roberts. Don't miss
Captivated, *Entranced* or *Charmed*. Only from
Silhouette Special Edition. . . .

COMING NEXT MONTH

AND BABY MAKES PERFECT
Mary Lynn Baxter

Ann Sinclair had a good reason for wanting to avoid sexy tycoon Drew MacMillan, but he wanted to see her again *and* he also wanted to stop the gossip about his virility!

JUST LIKE OLD TIMES
Jennifer Greene

Craig Reardon never understood what went wrong between him and his ex-wife, but he was trying to forget her until he realised that their old black magic was back. In fact, this time, *she* was seducing *him*!

MIDSUMMER MADNESS
Christine Rimmer

Plain Juliet Huddleston knew that sexy Cody McIntyre was way out of her league. But when he started noticing her, Juliet decided to trust her instincts—didn't she deserve a little romance?

COMING NEXT MONTH

SARAH AND THE STRANGER
Shawna Delacorte

Sarah Jane Morrison was assigned to help the most
gorgeous, sexy, stubborn, *blind* man she'd ever
seen. But everything else in Wade Danforth's life
was beautiful; how could Sarah Jane ever fit in?

A RESTLESS MAN
Lass Small

Creighton Brown had been sent on a rescue mission
by his family. Susanne Taylor, part of his extended
family, needed help and he'd been elected to go.
What could he do?

CONVENIENT HUSBAND
Joan Hohl

Stacy Hunsberger needed to make a deal with
Jasper Chance. He had no moral right to half her
farm, but he did have plenty of cash which she
desperately needed. Jasper though took one look at
Stacy and decided that it wasn't the farm he wanted!

COMING NEXT MONTH FROM

Sensation

*romance with a special mix of
suspense, glamour and drama*

THE HAVILAND TOUCH Kay Hooper
SONG OF THE MOURNING DOVE Lee Magner
MAN OF THE MOMENT Jackie Weger
BRADY'S LAW Mary Anne Wilson

Special Edition

*longer, satisfying romances with
mature heroines and lots of emotion*

THAT BOY FROM TRASH TOWN Billie Green
LUSCIOUS LADY Phyllis Halldorson
NOBODY'S BRIDE Judi Edwards
WEDDING EVE Betsy Johnson
WORLD'S GREATEST DAD Marie Ferrarella
CAPTIVATED Nora Roberts